OUTRUNNING *Crazy*

DEBORAH KIMMETT

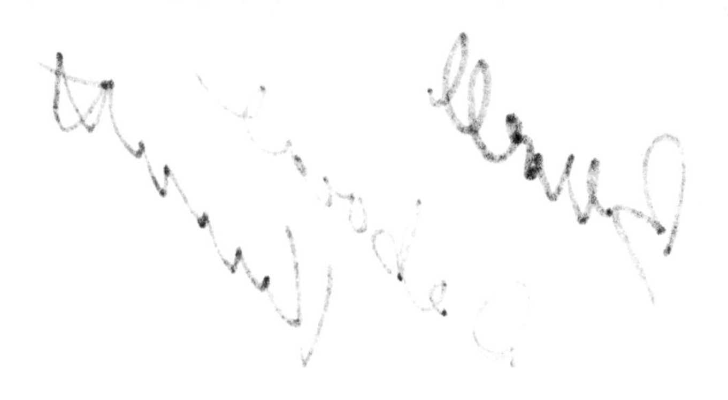

All characters appearing in this work are fictitious.
Any resemblance to real persons, living or dead,
is purely coincidental.

Cover Photo by Anez Poulos
Design by Hayley Dawn Designs

ACKNOWLEDGEMENTS

Many people held my hand, supported me and told me I could write this book. Thanks to Aysun Basaran, Sally Bowen, Lorna Willis, Deborah Dixon, Mary-Ellen Csamer, Rachel Atlas and Ruth Vandeberg. Special thanks goes to my two darling kids Brendan and Laurel Brady and my dear, dear dad Jim.

THE BIG PICTURE

The summer of 1968 is where my mind plops down and lights up a smoke. I remember when I was ten years old. It's hotter than Hades and we are standing in the woodshed, attached to the summer kitchen which smells like mouse shit and dried wood. There we all were, my siblings and my Mother standing in a woodshed, trying to outsmart one travelling salesman. On the particular day this salesman knocked until Alberta couldn't take it anymore and stormed out of our hiding place and asked him, "Jesus Mary and Joseph, what do you want?"

This guy was a simple slack-jawed man with an ugly church hat. When he took it off he introduced himself as Mr. Martin and looked straight ahead into Alberta's chest. He wasn't being fresh; he was short in stature. She was a bruiser of a woman, and when he peered through the screen, he was eyeball to eyeball with her substantial chest. Martin began his pitch on the other side of the screen door. "A few days ago, I flew over your property in my airplane and snapped some pictures of your land."

"What are you doing going around taking pictures of *my* land?" Alberta asked.

"Not your land in particular, ma'am. Everybody's land. I took pictures of all the farms in the neighbourhood."

"Why in the name of God would you do that?"

"It's beautiful to see the way things look from above, so far above everything. It gives you a whole new appreciation of what a blessing land can be."

"A blessing? My land?" Calling land a blessing revealed he didn't have a clue what it was like to be a farmer. Then he pulled the photographs from the manila envelope and handed them to her. There it was, our farm. Picture perfect, parceled off in rows, neat as a pin.

"See, what I do is I will take this picture and place it over a lampshade."

"A lampshade?" He pulled a small desk lamp out from his suitcase and placed our picture around it, attaching it with two clips so it would stick.

"Well, isn't that different?"

"Of course if you bought this it would be permanently placed on the shade. If you'd let me come in, I could plug it in, and you'd see how beautiful this looks when it's lit up."

Alberta unlatched the hook, grabbed the lamp, shut the screen door and re-hooked it before Martin even realized that he was still stuck out on the verandah.

"This contraption better not blow any fuses, or I won't be happy," she warned him.

"Full electrical grounding – it will stand a storm even out here in the middle of nowhere," he said, not knowing that calling a person's location nowhere is never a good sales move.

She bent over and plugged it in and when the lampshade lit up, he was right. It did look beautiful. It was odd to see our lives from that far up above things. All picture perfect.

"Well, that is different." Alberta said.

"Yes, ma'am. It's very reasonable for a beautiful piece of art."

"Art?" That word slapped her back to reality because she changed her tune right on the spot. "This is art? Why didn't you say so? Do I look like I have time for art? I'm a farmer."

She opened the screen door, handed it back to him, then hooked the lock again and exited to the woodshed, without so much as a good-bye or kiss my ass. When he heard Alberta start up the chainsaw in the back, Martin turned promptly on his heels and waddled down the driveway with his little penguin city boy walk, us kids in tow, yapping at him. It was my cousin Elaine who had the nerve to ask him: "Can we have the picture, can we Mister? Can we? Can we? Can we?"

He turned around quickly and raised his hand. It looked like he was going to hit her and then he dropped his shoulders in defeat. When he saw her pus-filled eyes, maybe he felt sorry for us, or maybe when he saw Alberta with a chain saw and safety goggles exiting the shed, he thought he'd walked into some back woods cult. Whatever it was, he offered up the picture to Elaine and said, "All right, all right, keep the dang thing. It's no use to me."

Then he placed his hat back on his head and he and the lamp disappeared down the road.

I've had that picture taped to the lamp in my bedroom for the past two years.

I took it with me when I moved to the apartment above the China Doll Restaurant and I brought it here to this place that where I sit looking back across the river. They say a picture never lies but this one did. When I stare at it I realize it didn't capture the truth about anything that was going on.

HOME

We grew up in Hawley – seven miles east of Spike's Junction, five miles north of nowhere on a land share where four generations from my mother's side had eked out a living. The red barns were in constant need of painting; a tractor stood in the middle of the cow pasture, stalled, left for years until a tree grew up around it. The cows used the rusted out seat as a salt lick.

My family lived in the stucco house which people called the *Old House*. It had been Nana Mary and JD's before they built their new ranch. Their abode had a wheelchair ramp because Nana was convinced she'd end up having a stroke.

Our place was run-down, nothing special to look at. The best room in the place was the summer kitchen right off the wood shed. It's where most of my good memories come from. An un-insulated extension off the regular part of the house, it was an architectural afterthought. It acted as a cold storage place for our baking in the winter. Easter weekend was when we moved everything from the larder in the regular kitchen to the cupboards in the summer one. During the summer months, we only used the rest of the house for sleeping.

I loved waking up on cold mornings in the spring when the frost had left but it was still chilly enough you had to pull the quilts up around your chin. The only thing that could pry me from bed was the smell of the woodstove burning. Alberta would have put the coffee pot on to perk and gone out to do the milking. There was nothing better than the smell of coffee perking on a wood stove. Tasting it was the real disappointment. It was dark and bitter so we had to load it up with Carnation milk and sugar. One sugar cube per teaspoon of coffee was the perfect ratio.

Alberta spent most of the summer packing a big pump of bug spray trying to win a war with black flies. She'd aim and fire it like an Uzi whether we were eating or not. The thing had so many pesticides it likely changed our genetic coding permanently. My mother Alberta was not someone you'd ever accuse of being affectionate. When she kissed us she made her lips flat, so there was no saliva. She was only nice if she thought you were retarded or dying. When I had the German measles my temperature spiked to 104° so I came close to the latter.

Out there in that summer kitchen she bathed me in cool water trying to get my fever to break, lying beside me all night, so I wouldn't go into convulsions.

I was lying on King's couch as Alberta brailed along my pockmarked skin with her hands that smelled like cow shit and Jergen's lotion, the smell I knew as mother.

I can still see her standing there in her see-through white cotton nightgown with pink flowered underpants peeking through as she sang to me off-key: "I ain't going to bed no more. I'm going to sleep on the hardwood floor. I'm a beeno." It is a tune she made up to make me happy, but when she sang it to me I thought I was dying.

Memory blurs time. I'm not sure if it was the same night, she was standing under the yellow hue of the bug light near the sink, shaving her legs. I see her balancing one of her legs when King came in from locking up his workshop for the day. As he stood there sipping his coffee, he watched her. They spoke in a soft way that reassures you when you're young. The content doesn't matter, just the sound of your parents' voices made you feel loved. She must've nicked herself because I remember hearing her yelling. "Dang it, King, I'm bleeding." He pulled a handkerchief out of his pocket, and started dabbing the spot where she was bleeding. "My God, lover, I've seen vets come back from Korea looking better than this." He then kissed her. I squinted to look as she swung her legs around and stood up and pulled him to her. Like the lamp salesman, King was short, so to kiss her he had to take off his shoes and stand on top of her feet.

I told myself she hated him, but I now know better. Her lips became full and red when he kissed her but she didn't like being that vulnerable. Sometimes after they smooched she looked like Bambi when his mother had been shot.

They'd grown up near each other, her on one side of the river and him on the other. They must have run into each other before but King liked to say the day he saw her first she was standing up at the front of a classroom bossing little children. At seventeen she was already a teacher, having graduated from Normal School. If anybody could've gone to a school to be normal it would've been Alberta for she was as practical a person as you could possibly meet. There was no dreaming in her blood.

Over six feet, one inch, she was so tall, if her height didn't intimidate the kids, her hollering would. The mouth on her could bring in cows from three fields back.

King had come to drop off his younger brother who was starting Grade One. He was bent over helping Robert tie up his shoes was when he first laid eyes on my mother. "Your mother's size thirteen feet came into view. I knew right then and there those pontoons would carry me to shore." He claimed he looked up, way up, and when he saw that pitch-black hair hanging down her back to her waist he knew she was a woman he could look up to. Being just under five six he was Sonny to her Cher.

King and the malarkey. He didn't have a serious bone in his body. He spent most of his life lying on the couch, cracking jokes. No matter how mad she got at him, no matter how much shit he got into every time she walked by, he'd slap her ass and every time she'd say, "No, King, not in front of the kids." And then she'd yell louder, "Not in front of the kids", and then a few months later there'd be another baby.

He didn't give her an engagement ring for two more years after they met. For one thing he had to save for it. And two, Babcock men are like that. They'd go around with a person forever before they'd commit themselves. King went to a consignment sale the jewelry store was having and even convinced Suitcase Ray to let him have the ring before it had been paid off. I think he still owes money on it. He gave her the engagement ring on a Thursday night, and legend has it that when he got up the next morning, Grandma Babcock, his mother had poached him a couple of eggs.

"You won't be eating any more meat on Friday," she said, as she put the plate in front of him. "She's a Cochrane. Cochranes are Catholic, to the core." Everybody knew he'd convert; there was no way around it. At St Paul's Church, they got married on a windy day in October, the kind of day where people have to hold on to their hats.

I was born nine and a half months later, making a dramatic entrance. She had wanted to be one of those women who went out to the field, popped out a kid, and was back on her feet before the end of the day. Obviously I didn't get the memo because I was born three weeks late, lollygagging around inside of her like I'd walked in there and forgotten what I went in for.

"What were you doing in there?" my mother asked me

over and over again as she showed me her Cesarean scar one more time. She waited and waited and waited until one day after she had a feed of liver and onions, she couldn't quit belching. King said he knew right off that it was time for a baby to be born but she never listened to him because he was a damn man. After ten hours of belching and farting around she called the doctor, and he agreed with King's prognosis. "You're in labour, but the baby is in the wrong position so you'll have to go in for a C-section."

After thirteen hours and 300 dollars paid, I made my debut. All that time and money for something she felt she could have done at home. "The other kids knew enough to come out when they were supposed to, but not you."

A lot of kids liked hearing their birth stories, but I didn't.

King named me. He took one look at me and called me Tammy from that movie with Debbie Whatsername. I've since changed it to Tamara, but nobody in my family will call me that. They say I am being a big phony. "Your name is Tammy, it says so on your birth certificate." Of course when I asked where my birth certificate was, Alberta claimed she couldn't find it. I always longed to be adopted, to have royalty for parents, but no such luck as my mother's face is pasted on mine.

I was round, plump and colicky. For six months I blatted like a calf. King bragged he was the only one who could settle me. He'd spend half the night walking the floors with me carrying on. He'd stick me up under his armpit, and I'd pass out. His pits smelled like sweet cut onion. When Alberta came out in the morning, we'd be nestled there together on the couch.

King had trouble with regular work. At school when they asked me to write down what my father did for a living, I needed extra foolscaps. There's just about nothing he didn't do. Over his lifetime, he has run a mobile park, operated a bulldozer, a dump truck, and a front-end loader. He worked for the MTO one winter driving a snowplow.

There wasn't anything he wouldn't try. Once he tried his hand at being a blacksmith, but that was an expensive proposition because after he bought the horse he then never took the time to break it. It ran all over the neighborhood jumping fences. I can still see us chasing that damn thing down the side road, calling after it, showing everyone we didn't have a clue. Finally Alberta sent it away to the gelatin factory. I tried boycotting Jell-O when she told me, tried imagining pony knuckle stirred into the Cool Whip, but I have no self-control. All I did was eat it faster so I wouldn't think about what I was consuming.

My father was a great starter, but got bored easy. He had a head full of ideas, all of them bad. One of his all-time bad ideas is the reason we ended up back at the farm.

Alberta quit teaching soon after I came along. They had moved into their apartment in town, a love nest is what King said he called it. It was a one-room apartment with the bathtub down the hall. Alberta had been looking in the paper dreaming about them buying a house some day. She was just noodling out loud, but by the end of the week King had bought them one at an auction.

Alberta found out about it by chance when she went into McGrath's Clothing Store to buy herself some shoes. She had been saving the baby bonus cheque for three months. Marj, the clerk, said, "I heard King went and bought the Findlay house."

"I don't think so." Alberta hadn't learned yet to keep her mouth shut until she got more information.

"Well, I heard it this morning when I went over to the diner for coffee. People there were surprised. It looks like it's a surprise to you, too?"

Alberta scooted out of the store and when she opened their apartment door, he was sitting there in the La-Z-Boy in his green flood pants, hunched over. Whenever he was going to catch shit, he sat forward on his knees like he couldn't catch his breath.

"How was your day, King?" she asked.

"I did the damnedest thing." That's all he had to say before she would go ape shit, and say the same thing every time.

"My God. What were you thinking?" That sentence should be written on her tombstone.

Alberta went back to Nana and JD and they were waiting for her. It's like they lived for this. Watching their kids screw up made them feel better about their own lives.

There they sat, all afternoon, giving Alberta advice. Un-helpful sayings like '*you made your bed, now you can lie in it.*' When they got through raking her over the coals, they did what they always did, they bailed her out. JD went to the Findlays and offered one of his best spring calves if they would just forget about the whole thing. He lost the deposit, which meant he had to cover the cheque, but he got King out of the deal. No bounced cheque, so he saved face. The Findlays forgave the rest of the matter. They may have forgotten but J.D. didn't. That man would never give anybody something for nothing. He told Alberta she'd have to come home and move into the old farmhouse. He'd fund her to get some more milking cows. Since the two of them were young and with the right focus, they could make a go of it. He and Nana started building their dream house and no, he didn't give her the farm outright. He was afraid King would screw up that deal, so he leased it to her like she was an indentured servant. She had all the responsibility and none of the freedom. For a long time she claimed that she didn't mind at all, but that's what people say when they're forced into doing something they don't want to do.

My mother's and my life were similar in that we both went ass over teakettle before we hit twenty. I was nine months old when we moved back to the farm. I took one look at it and broke out in a rash.

COWS

The land we farmed should have been ashamed of itself. Peppered with gristle and sweat, it managed to cough up some hay and measly balls of evergreen and some root vegetables. In the spring Columbine grew amidst the stone. I thought it was pretty. I transplanted it to fertile soil in the garden next to the house, but it died from too much attention. Even the flowers needed to be ignored. Our family was into cattle. JD was what they called a drover. It's an old-fashioned term for a man who buys and sells cattle off the end of his truck. He'd pull up and make an offer to a farmer, and then take the same cow down the road and sell it to another farmer for a profit. Cattle rustling was how he got rich during the depression. He always had a few head of dairy cattle, but when Alberta came back they decided to make it a bigger operation. She started milking 80 cows morning and night – winter, summer, death or birth. During hard times and good those cows needed to be milked. You can be crazy or good as gold, it really doesn't matter to cows. They need to be milked at the same time day in and day out. The predictability is mind numbing. Your knees give out before your determination. To get out of gym class, other girls would say they got their periods but I'd tell them my knees were bruised and bothered. Whenever I met new friends, I told them we milked two hundred head, as if exaggerating how many milking cows you had could ever impress a person. Saying you're a farmer doesn't incite jealousy in anybody. Most people think farmers are thick. Farmers even say it about each other. People in town talked slow to us like we didn't understand what they were saying. I found out pretty quickly that if I played stupid, they shut up faster – especially the government guys, the ones from the milk marketing board.

They started regulating our milk prices when I was seven. I hit the age of reason at the same time Alberta had to buy quota. Quota is a hard concept for most people to get. What it boils down to is a farmer buys the right to milk his own cows. If we wanted to milk a lot of cows, we had to buy a lot of quota. This keeps prices consistent and gives you a regular pay cheque. But the quota is really worth nothing until you sell. That's farming. You get rich once you get out of it. You make more money when you stop doing it. A lot like insurance, you're worth more dead than alive.

The drawback comes when there are a few good cows that produce more milk than you bought quota for. If you overproduce, you either have to dump the milk or make a lot of ice cream and butter. You don't want to have to call the milk truck guy to take it away because he'd charge you to take your own milk. They charged you for that plus charged you what you would have been paid. You want a cow that is a good producer; however, if you buy more quota you make more money. But then there's pressure because the cow has to keep up its end of the bargain and keep producing milk over the long haul, or the marketing board will fine you because you're not producing enough. I did my science project on this once, and I got a D because the teacher said the whole thing didn't make a bit of sense. Alberta was furious. She wrote a note back to the teacher saying if it doesn't make sense to *you*, how do you think *we* feel?

Alberta bent over backwards trying to inspire my father to work with her, to help him get on the same team. She tried to let him go to auction for cattle but King would have no part of it. He had a hate-on for cows that apparently started when he was a little boy. He claimed the cows attacked him once in the back field but when he brought his father out to prove it to him, the cows stood there acting docile and dumb.

He would tell my mother he'd love to help farm but she was raising the wrong livestock. The pig was a far superior animal. So to please him, she bought thirty of them for his twenty-first birthday. Didn't he love telling anybody that would listen that he was into pork bellies? Nana gave him an annual subscription to the Farmer's Almanac for that same birthday which was a mistake because it was in there that he found an article about a guy down south who penned all his hogs on a bus.

One day when no one was watching him, he went into town and bought a school bus to put the pigs in. Alberta's head must have nearly blown off when she came out in the morning and saw a bus on the lawn with thirty damn pigs in it. Within a month, the stupid things had eaten all the seats. People laughed at him – even JD thought it was funny. But Alberta didn't crack a smile. They had their one and only fight.

King blew up and said, "I can't do anything to please you, can I Alberta?"

Alberta said, "I guess not."

Then he said that maybe he should just stay out of her business and she should stay out of his. Alberta agreed and she hired a tow truck to take the bus to the dump. They killed the pigs, and we ate pork chops all winter. From then on the cheques from the Marketing Board were deposited directly to her farm account. Whenever we would ask King for an allowance, he would point to Alberta, "You have to consult the boss at head office."

King didn't lie down and play dead. He learned to stay under the radar. It was the best way to keep the peace. Nana loved him because he called her sweetheart and told her she still looked good in short shorts. His compliments got her to give him money to convert the drive shed into a mechanic's shop. He named it *King's Repair and Repartee Shop.*

He sat out there even in the dead of winter, heating the place with an old oil furnace he had pilfered from the dump. He ran it from the used motor oil he drained from cars. Reused oil gets the job done, but it's filthy and practically chokes the life out of you, but the men that came in for a sit and chew didn't seem to notice. He would fix their sump pumps and small engines and made just enough money the taxman didn't notice.

He held court with folks from three counties over. I used to think my dad was the mayor because when we went downtown he waved at everybody. He had an opinion on everything. There wasn't one subject he didn't know something about and if he didn't, he'd spend all night reading from the Books of Knowledge he bought from another of the traveling salesmen. He loved to quote Will Rogers and Mark Twain. When I was a kid, I thought he made up those wise sayings because he never gave them credit. The men who came to his shop were a bunch of his cousins who hung off every word he said. Slow-talking men who took so long to answer, sometimes you thought they might have died. They asked him where he learned, what he learned, and he would say he got his education at the University of Chicago. This was a bunch of baloney too because he never went to high school let alone the States. But when adults tell big stories, they are not called liars, they are called *characters*. On our property there were three houses with a whole bunch of characters.

NANA

Great Grandma Jib who lived in County Galway, Ireland, got mad at her husband for lipping off one too many times and when no one was looking socked enough money away to buy a one-way ticket to Canada. On that trip, while everybody below was puking and hanging on for dear life, she started courting one of the deck hands. He was the one who eventually became Nana's father. This new man was called up to duty for WW1, three months after they landed in Canada. Nana never met her Dad because he went overseas and got killed a few weeks before she was born. This elevated him to saint status, because he died before anybody found out what was wrong with him.

'A man you know little about is the best man of all.'

That's what Nana's sister, Great Aunt Margaret, used to say. She ran away too, because her husband turned out to be gay, which I don't think bothered her until she caught him with her undergarments on. He was a big man in the shoulders so she could never get the bras to go back to their regular size.

Then there was Launa, Alberta's oldest sister. She moved into town and married a fireman. But she ran off Uncle Gary before long and most people think it was because of her miniatures collection. She loved the miniature people sitting on miniature chairs on top of miniature doilies perched on miniature shelves inside of miniature cupboards. You couldn't take one step without running into them. Uncle Gary was a big, clumsy man and he kept knocking them off the shelf. Finally he left and went back home to live with his mother so he could put his feet up.

You couldn't tease Launa about the miniatures. She was one of those people with no sense of humour. We went to her house years after Gary had left, and some of the little baby dolls had fallen over in a little bowl of blueberries. Launa fiddled with them so much that the lunch she was serving got cold. Mom finally asked if the dolls would like to have lunch with them and Launa shot her a look like Medusa.

Alberta asked, "What are you going to do to me, Launa? Turn me into one of your porcelain entities?"

Launa still hasn't changed much. She got herself a new man who she meets in a motel room once a week, a man who told her off the top he would never leave his wife which she said suited her fine. She doesn't have to worry about him tramping through her house breaking anything.

Nana kept up the tradition but she didn't run too far, just across the field to our house.

After she got into her new house, people thought she'd settle down. It had brand-new everything. The kitchen had an island and a new olive green fridge and stove.

JD and Nana were fine separately but together they were miserable. All they did was fight. In the old days, Alberta used to go over to their place to referee. "What is wrong with you two?" she'd ask.

"I asked him to take me into town tomorrow to do my shopping. But he won't stop watching Gunsmoke."

That made JD grunt and turn the TV up even louder.

"Miss Kitty never bothers Matt Dillon for money, does she?" JD would say this as if it was proof of something.

"It's my egg money, old man," Nana retorted and hit him with her broom.

"She takes my money and goes to the track," JD snapped back.

Boots had taken her once years ago before he lost his license, and JD still wouldn't let it go. Nana hit him again.

"Mother, stop it," said Alberta. "When are you two going to get along? Eh?"

Nana looked at JD. "Well, answer her. She asked when you're going to get along with me, old man." At this point, JD would do something ignorant like lift his leg and let go a cracker jack of a fart.

Nana would then pitch a hairy fit. "That's it. Alberta, take me to the bus station."

She had never learned to drive so she spent more time in the back of a bus than most people. In the early days, she'd go to stay with her brother, Father Don, or go down to the States to see the two American sisters. Over the years, they got sick of her bellyaching so after a while she wasn't welcome there any more.

"Mother, you're not going on any bus," Alberta would object every time like this was the first time she had ever heard of her mother doing a crazy thing.

"Well, I'll go to town and stay with Launa then," said Nana. But she hated Launa because she was mealy-mouthed. Being pale and scrawny like a tomcat didn't add to her good qualities either.

"Or I could go to Berle's." Nana would never go there because that house smelled. Every house had a distinct odour. Ours smelled like coffee. Nana's smelled like Glade. Elaine's smelled like raw meat. Berle's house stank like wet hound.

Berle's kids were encouraged so much that everybody

was sure they'd turn out to be criminals but despite the excessive praise, they were actually the nicest bunch in the lot.

That's how Nana always ended up with us. We annoyed her least. When you're running away, you want less stress, not more. Every few weeks, I'd wake up and she'd be lying beside me in bed snoring. I stared at her when she slept. You could see a young person trying to escape from behind the closed eyelids. The red lipstick was never cleaned off her lips. There was a permanent curvy line painted above her lip, slightly off the mark because she used a wooden match to apply it.

She wore plastic shoes with hot pants and black pantyhose to church where she'd accuse the men taking up the collection of wanting to pinch her backside. She looked older than Jesus. One time in church, I thought she was wearing knee high pantyhose so I went to pull it up, but it was the skin on her leg.

She had no hair to speak of so she bought a batch of wigs, which she called *Zelda* – after the writer F. Scott Fitzgerald's wife. She never read any of his books but she said she liked the sound of the letter 'zed.'

If you went into her walk-in closet, you would see the wigs lined up in a row, perched on Styrofoam heads with no eyes or lips. It was a terrifying sight, especially when we were stoned. My cousin Elaine and I smoked up once and we were sure the things were talking to us.

Nana put a piece of pantyhose on her head so no stray hairs would peak out, then she'd place Zelda on top. It was not a subtle wig. There was a lot of hair on top of her head. She was about three inches taller when she wore it When she took it off, her head looked too small for her body, like you'd put a Barbie doll head on a baby doll's body. I have one picture of her looking like that from when she was in the hospital. Alberta gave it to me and said, "This is what she really looked like. That's my real mother. If only she had just once tried being herself."

I'd try to avoid housework by hiding out with Nana in the living room. She was the only one allowed to watch TV in the middle of the day. We'd sit in there eating Peppermint Patties with the drapes closed so the sun wouldn't fade the upholstery

"You got any titties?" She pinched my chest.

"Ow."

"Stop your hollering. There isn't anything there to be screaming about, yet. They're mosquito bites. When they start sprouting, you won't know what hit you. I was musical before I had breasts. I played the piano which kept me out of trouble until I was nearly nineteen."

"You didn't get breasts until you were nineteen?" I asked.

"Well, I was a late bloomer. The music was good for me. I started to go into the town Furlong to play for the Catholic League's Socials. Reach there in the cedar chest for my smokes."

"Mom doesn't want you smoking in here."

She ignored me and reached her hand out for her Peter Jackson's, pulled one out and lit it.

"I had gone down to Furlong playing piano at the priests' social for St. Patrick's Day."

Nana could play a mean piano, had learned all the jigs everybody wanted to hear. Even though she only played at church socials, on the night she and JD met, everybody was drinking green beer. JD walked in.

She took a drag off her smoke and exhaled the same story. "That Man was young then. He looked mysterious and messy, like an Italian, but he was an Irish through and through. Hair all-greased back with bear wax and way too long in the front. He had to keep flipping his head back to keep it out of his eyes." She growled like a tiger.

"I sat there playing the piano wearing one of those shirts. What do you call it? Right there. I was wearing it in that picture." She pointed to the photo sitting on the bookshelf, the picture taken when she was sixteen or seventeen.

"A peasant blouse," I responded.

"Yes. Look at me there. I acted like I knew something. I knew nothing. I liked the attention from the men, but I never did anything to encourage them. I felt safe inside myself until I saw That Man. A feeling came over me up from the roots of my being. It was like everything was slowed down, and suddenly I was an ornament on a mantle."

I imagined a halo around her piano with a light streaming down from heaven. There she was, playing like an innocent cherub until That Man entered the room. That Man changed her in That Way that made her thin fingers become fat and clumsy.

With the cigarette hanging from her mouth, she sucked the smoke in deep until it reached down to the bottom of her slippers. Slow plumes of smoke wafted through the room and hit the window. Dormant flies stirred from their sleep.

"John Daniels had come down from the north to make his way in cattle."

"Who's John Daniels?" I asked.

"That Man never held my hand, never kissed me, or looked into my eyes the way you hear how some men do. One night he drove me back to our farm and walked me to the house. Before I knew it, he'd pushed me up against the door. I could feel his heart beating. It was all hard in his pants, and I could feel myself go damp down there." She pointed to *down there,* and I quickly covered myself in case she was going to do more pinching.

"I didn't know what was happening to me. I wanted to kiss him. I'd never kissed a man before. But when I brought my lips up to his, he said if I ever made him do anything before we got married, he'd never respect me. See, with him, it was all or nothing. You know what I mean?"

"No."

"Good, and don't you find out, or I'll tan your backside. That was that. We got married the next week."

"You only knew Grandpa for a week?" I was taken aback.

"It's like living in dog years when you're in that way. She leaned toward me blowing smoke in my face. "I'm talking about spontaneous combustion. Of course, I had no idea what I was in for. I waited until we got married, but still I got no respect. He's always treated me like I was dirty. If I made any noise or laughed when we were in the boudoir, he'd tell me I was a...."

Alberta's shadow in the doorway stopped further explanation. Nana quickly handed me the cigarette; I butted it out against my shoe.

Alberta asked, "Telling you, you were a what, Mother?"

"Nothin'."

"Oh something, Mother, it's always something. What were you telling the girl?"

"I don't remember," Nana said.

"Yes you do."

Nana glared at Alberta. "No, I don't. Maybe I have crème de mentia."

"Cripes, you're too young for dementia. .... And what are *you* doing sitting around in here in the middle of a beautiful sunny day." Alberta had turned her attention to me.

"I'm entertaining her...." I stammered.

"Tammy, if you have time to be entertaining someone, you have time enough to go hang out the laundry." That was Alberta logic. She hated seeing anyone sitting around enjoying themselves.

"Mother, how many times do I have to tell you not to smoke in the good living room?"

Alberta quickly left and went out to the kitchen to get the Glade air freshener. She started spraying it at her mother, until she had no choice but to call That Man to come and get her.

When she'd dial JD would answer on the first ring. Neither one of them ever said hello to each other. "Yeah, it's me. Yeah. Have you smartened up yet? Uh huh? Uh huh? I don't know where it is. Are you blind, old man? Use your eyes. Look in the larder. I cooked it before I left. Honest to God. Hurry up and come and get me before you starve to death."

There was a long pause.

"Do you know where I am?" Nana asked.

This cracked me up. Of course he knew where she was. He could probably see her from his front step. He walked out to the verandah, got in the car and drove down his driveway and up ours. I'd be standing outside looking like I was doing something useful when he put the car in park and gave me a salute.

"How you doin', Suzie?" He called all of his granddaughters Suzie. We were interchangeable to him.

Then he'd honk the horn. Nana appeared in the doorway with her oversized sunhat, holding Zelda, the wig, on its white Styrofoam head like it was a child being dragged between homes. Even though she was walking right towards him, he'd lay on the horn again. "Come on, I haven't got all day," he yelled.

"Hold your horses." She turned to me and winked like she'd won some kind of battle; then she would kiss me on the top of my head and said words that baffled me. "Don't be a stranger, pet."

"I won't," I said.

How could I be a stranger when she never stayed at home?

BOOTS

King came down with us in the evening to the river but he woudn't swim. His side of the family didn't believe in getting wet. King would make a thermos of instant coffee from the A&P for him and the ladies. "Me and my harem," he said to Aunt Lillian. He claimed if you drank caffeine in the summer, it wouldn't keep you awake, that the heat would counteract it the way a salad counteracts the calories of a burger. The adults had big mugs of the stuff and he and my mother would cuddle up on the lounge chair with him tucked up between Alberta's tree trunk legs. It might've been called a date if they hadn't been surrounded by a posse of kids. They smooched like they were newlyweds.

Lillian sat away from them to give them privacy. She sat closer to the water, in the open wind, perched on that blue camp chair of hers, staring out. Her brain was a snowstorm of worry but still that smile was pasted on her puss.

Three adults trying to count heads; six kids swimming. Elaine went everywhere with her dog, Reg, who barked like an idiot every time one of us put our head under the water.

As an only child, Elaine would holler at her mother a hundred times a night. “Mom, look at me. Look at me. Mom, are you looking? Watch. Oh no, not that one. I didn’t do it right. Watch. Okay? Watch us. Mom, please watch me. No. Not that time.”

If we had made a racket like that, we would’ve been told to ‘go the hell home’but Lillian just sat there and said, “My landsake, I am watching, Elaine. I know you can swim.”

We swam until our lungs hurt and our lips were blue chattering. *No we’re not cold. We don’t’ want to go, not yet. Please, ten more minutes*. We’d only have to come out when it was too dark for the adults to see us. Some nights King would build a campfire, and Lillian would bring marshmallows and hot dogs –with real buns. We always had to put our wieners on bread.

King would tell us one of his big stories. My favourite was about ‘Tom the Turkey.’

It was a sad story about when my dad was a boy. Nobody wanted him to have a turkey as a pet. They’re not bright birds and Tom was no exception. He was so dense that he thought he was a chicken, but the chickens hated him. They gave him a rough time for playing the big shot, eating their food.

One day one of the big capons, a real mean one, pecked him right out of the coop, right into the pig slough. That year Tom ended up being the Thanksgiving bird, but he didn’t die in the way you might think. He died of natural causes. One day it started to rain and when the water began hitting him on the head, he looked up and opened his mouth in amazement. “Uh duh, where’s that water coming from? Is the sky leaking?”

King delivered the punch line with his Tom the turkey voice, slow and dense. “Tom stood there, his head pointed up toward the sky in a trance, slack-jawed until he drowned. That’s how Tom, ended ......up...” Then his face caved in on top of itself, and he couldn’t get to the punch line. He’d be shaking to the bones, and we’d scream, “Daddy, finish the story, finish the story..." And then he'd say, "Ended up on the table...."

King would collapse and roll all over the ground, laughing like a moron. All us kids would jump on him and he'd tickle us.

"Tell it again Daddy, tell it again," we'd all chant.

Alberta would say, "No, that's enough." To her nobody gained anything by doing something over and over again. She ate oranges once a year at Christmas when they were in season. She played Elvis records only on Elvis's birthday, and only let Daddy tell his stories once. It was important to keep memories special.

When the mosquitoes had practically eaten us all alive, we packed up the chairs and walked back to where we had parked our vehicle. Crickets and frogs croaked out a symphony. The boys and Elaine ran around snapping each other with their wet towels. I'd have Marley on my shoulders because the kid was terrified of walking on wet grass because of the snakes.

Many a night he'd appear out of thin air. Like an apparition, Boots stepped out from the cluster of trees, a cigarette balanced on his bottom lip. The ember identified him as my Uncle Boots. This was my mother's brother, a hulk of a man with broad shoulders; beside him my mother looked petite.

One time she yelled at him. "Why do you sneak up on us like that?" He went ballistic and garbled horrible cuss words at her that he didn't spell. Boots never managed to speak English with full, comprehensible sentences, only baffled, muddled tones.

King, who would do anything to keep the peace, said, "Alberta, you're only making it worse." He knew Boots was drunk and there was no point in arguing. The man was just there to round up his family. The man's personality loomed over every event on that side of the family. If Lillian and

Elaine attended we knew he'd show up sometime during the night. Wedding and baby showers, any place where women wore pie plates with bows, he'd have to ruin. We'd be playing a party game and he'd appear on the verandah and stare at the screen door watching us, not saying anything.

Elaine would sense him before anyone else. Since she was a little girl, she understood timing. She wore a pink watch, the one with leather straps that never lost time. Elaine got so good at knowing when he was there, she wouldn't even have to see him. The hair on her back would go up. I watched her back arch. They were connected to each other by electrical currents like the ones that run under the barn to keep the cows warm in the winter.

She would give her mother a signal and they would start gathering up their sweaters. She'd move around the room, kiss the relatives, wish the one wearing the paper plate with the bows on her head good luck and they'd call it a night.

Lillian had the title of her mother, but she didn't seem to know what her job description was. She'd smile her phony smile and ask like a little girl, "Do we have to go already, Elaine?"

Elaine would say, "Yes, Mother, we do, now!"

"Well I guess she's right. How did this kid of mine get so smart?"

Lost Lillian we called her as she muttered her good-byes. Muttering about how she had a lovely time and she better get a move on. *Boots had to go to bed. Boots had to get up in the morning. He's got a pile of orders ahead of him.*

We were a noisy people. The kind of people you wouldn't want to camp next to. We yelled when we were trying to be friendly and yelled when we were mad. if volume was any indicator for a storm brewing to most families, it wasn't for us. We had no volume control, not much could silence us. Except for him.

When Boots appeared out of the woods, we stopped

dead in our tracks. We were like animals on high alert. No one made any sudden moves. We watched them as they climbed into the truck. The passenger door needed oil. Even in the terrible state he was in, Lillian would let him drive. All the women I knew did this- let their man drive drunk. Didn't want to ruffle any feathers. He was so plastered he couldn't get the key in the ignition. After several failed attempts he eventually stopped trying swearing under his breath he'd throw the cigarette butt out the window and rest his head on the steering wheel until he got his second wind.

As they pulled away, Elaine sat on the folded down tailgate holding onto Reg, hair wet, pulling the dog close so he wouldn't fall. She turned on the flashlight and put it up to her face so she looked insane. She was trying to make us laugh because she knew he couldn't see her. That was Elaine- she knew about timing - when to make a joke and when it was time to pull back from the edge

ELAINE

Elaine and I had karma from the get-go. From the start it was like we were working something out from a previous life. Maybe we had been twins in the city of Atlantis. Or she had killed my cat during the occupation of Japan. I imagine us tumbling towards our present incarnations – cartoon seeds with scrawny arms free-falling towards earth. We were both aiming for Alberta, knowing that side of the fence was the best of a bad choice. She elbowed me. I elbowed her. Kapow. She ended up on the bad side and me on the good.

From the day I was born, I was told I was from the good family. I think they put it in the birth announcement in the paper. Tammy Babcock, born to a better family. She'd better stop her bitching. She'd better count her blessings. As it turned out, neither side was much to write home about. I wasn't some queen and she my servant. Circumstances turned out to be surprisingly similar. Neither of us was too far above or too far below the other. Which made things crazier in a way. We were on one big teeter-totter. One minute I was on top and then the next minute she would take off and I would fall to earth.

The grievances I had against her would never hold up in some karma court but I will list them all the same.

She didn't have enough originality to be born in a different year so we ended up in the same grade all throughout school. We'd just started grade one and the two of us had come inside from the first recess of our lives. I remember I was dressed in a long sleeved shirt and thick beige-coloured leotards. It was still hot that September, but Psoriatics all over the planet wear thick uncomfortable clothing even in the middle of a heat wave. They don't want people to notice their red spots. We sat down at our new desks and I rolled up my sleeves to start learning to print. Tongue out to balance the pencil just right. I had been up all night throwing up, sure that other kids were going to learn how to spell before me, when Elaine yelled out at the top of her lungs, "Is that the chicken pox, Tammy?" She said it deliberately. She knew everybody had been worried about my skin since I was an infant. My skin ailments weren't a family secret. Obviously she had been holding a grudge from another lifetime, otherwise why would she have said it so loud over and over again in front of the entire class? I tried being patient with her for a while.

At the next recess, she did it again. "Is that chicken-pox all over you, Tammy?"

I put up with her nonsense for two days until I lost it and took a baseball bat and lambasted her. Mrs. Harris made me stay in at recess and print out – '*I must not hit people with baseball bats*.' A hundred times she made me print it, until I got the heartbreak of arthritis.

Elizabeth Dowdle, who was in grade eight and stout at the time because of the thyroid, sidled up to me on the bus and whispered, "Ignore the ignorant." A very good piece of advice, but near impossible to do as Elizabeth found out when she volunteered to supervise my tenth birthday party.

I had to invite Elaine. All the cousins were coming so there was no avoiding it. I was incredibly nervous to begin with, as we didn't get a party every year like some of my town cousins did. With five kids wanting to celebrate, Alberta said she would have gone bananas baking cakes every time she turned around. So we got a celebration once every five years and that meant there was a lot of pressure for it to be perfect.

I came up with the brilliant idea of a sleepover down by the river. Alberta had first threatened to camp out with us but that would've been a disaster, as she would've made us go to bed an hour after dark. (The only point of a sleepover is to sleep when it's over.) I told Elizabeth and she must've felt sorry for me because she offered to help.

Elaine arrived late, making a grand entrance wearing only her bikini. She waltzed down to the campsite flaunting her smooth skin, hips swaying like she was some kind of fashion model .

I was entertaining people. I say this humbly but I was a clever child. I had created my own language and I was teaching my guests a new word – 'Sconfatisha' – that meant peachy keen.

Everyone knew I was having fun but this word play annoyed Elaine. She proceeded to tear off her bathing suit.

"It's time to skinny dip."

It was still light out but she took her clothes off in broad daylight.

Psoriatics generally don't skinny dip. You would never see one of us at a nudist camp.

I responded with something quite mature like, "It's my party and we have to do what I say." Whatever I might have said, nobody listened to *me*, the red spotted birthday girl in a one-piece bathing suit with a full body caftan cover-up. No, they stripped down to the buff and jumped into the river while I sat there with Elizabeth, who was far too fat for nudity.

Once they all finished their nonsense, Elaine put on

quite a show, getting everyone to sing to me and give me the Royal Bumps. After my backside had welts, she insisted I open my gifts – I got Evening in Paris powder, a purple smiley face pillow and an Ouija Board from the Hellion of the ball. Devil worship is what Lillian would've called it today, but she was the one who bought it for me. After dark around the campfire, we stuck our hands on the board and asked it questions, and it started to move around the letters, spelling out the word G.H.O.S.T. Elizabeth said 'Elaine is controlling the board'. Of course she denied it, claiming that the devil himself was making it move. Didn't that get everybody going. They all started screaming that they wanted to go back and sleep in the house. Elizabeth told her to shut her gob because she was getting everyone worked up, but Elaine wouldn't let it go. She claimed she had read in her mother's *True Confessions* magazine that you could get possessed while you're sleeping. "The devil can climb up under your flannelette nightgown and take over your soul."

"I don't want to be possessed by the devil," Amy cried – as if anybody would.

Elaine started rolling on the ground making spit come out of the side of her mouth and the girls were screaming so much Elizabeth had to go over her and slap Elaine across the head.

"Shut up, right this instant," said Elizabeth and Elaine stayed still on the ground and got a demented look on her face and rolled around in the dirt. When everybody was at the peak of hysteria, she stood up and started laughing at us.

"Suckers! Only suckers believe in demonic possession!" Then she climbed in the sleeping bag and rolled over and went to sleep.

That's Elaine for you. She could stir things up and still sleep like a log. I calmed them all with one of Dad's crazy animal stories and eventually they all nodded off, whimpering in their sleep – filling the tent with sounds of whistling snores.

I lay there wide-awake, worried sick that if I dozed off, the devil would climb into my underpants.

Another thing that bugged me about her was there wasn't one special occasion she didn't try to hone in on. All she wanted was some attention but I was jealous of her affect on people, especially my father.

He had a soft spot for her. King had rented an ice cream truck – it was one of the best bad ideas he had. That summer he had to deliver gallons of ice cream to general stores for a sixty-mile radius. We'd drive around Hawley, from Fredricksburgh to Addington up to Sills Junction and Buck Lake. There were fourteen stores in total. In the hot weather, the route might take all day because the storeowners ordered more ice cream when there were cottagers. With nearly two hundred tubs to deliver, he asked me to help him out. When you're the oldest of five kids, it's a big deal to get a private audience with your parents, so this was my opportunity to be his favourite. We had to leave before dawn so I could get back home in time for the night milking. As far as Pope Alberta was concerned nothing got me speical dispensation from milking. So, I would wake up earlier than him. I see him on the couch, snoring like Fred Flintstone. Quietly I would light the stove in the summer kitchen to get the dampness out of the air and tip-toe around trying to make our lunch: bologna sandwiches with Miracle Whip. By the time he came to, I had our lunches and a thermos of coffee ready.

After a quick breakfast, King would back the truck out of his shed and I'd climb in and he would sit with his coffee cup. Then he'd roll down the driver's window a crack, and light up a smoke. I'd roll down my window, and light up a Popeye cigarette. It had red on the end so it looked real. I'd suck. He'd suck. We'd both suck. He'd try to find something good on the radio.

"What kind of music would you like, Tammy? Country or Western?"

"I think Western."

"Well, Country it is then."

It was our joke and he'd turn the dial until he brought in the channel.

Thinking about those mornings is like ginger ale. It bubbles up through my nose and makes me cry. I felt urgent when I was with him, like any day the world would discover his genius and I would have no father. So, I prepared for our field trips like I was auditioning for him. I wanted him be proud that he had a smart daughter like me. I would read the newspaper and save my important questions all week for him, big-thinker questions that would show him exactly how advanced my mind could be. He would listen to me go on, laughing and being impressed in the right places, then he'd shake his head and say, "Yer mouth is running like a whip-poor-will's ass," which he meant as a compliment. I think.

But the honeymoon period was soon over. After about three Saturdays of father- daughter bliss, we pulled out of our driveway one morning and there she was standing at the end of hers. Elaine stood in the grove of trees wearing only a sleeveless shirt and a pair of shorts – short shorts with no bum cups hanging below. Her mother was asleep in their car, at the end of the driveway. When Elaine saw us, she tapped her watch like we were late. King pulled up beside her and rolled down the window.

"What are you doing, out here 'Lainy?"

"Waiting for you. You are thirteen minutes behind schedule. You've got over 140 miles to cover today so you don't want to get behind from the get-go."

King looked up toward her house and we both saw Boots standing at the window, holding a Red Cap in his hand, his belly hanging over his belt like a burp. "Okay, hop in, Lainy, yer making me cold just looking at you."

Elaine tried to push me over so she could get the window seat, but I put my feet out to block her. She karate-chopped my legs when I wouldn't give in; she eventually had to climb over me. There were brown hooks hanging down on her white skin.

"Your underwear has knobs," I said.

"It's not underwear. It's my girdle."

"What the heck you got a girdle on for?"

"I'm a slouch. With a girdle on, I have to sit up straight, or I get a big wedgie on my stomach."

"Where on earth did you get the girdle?" King asked. Everything she said or did, he thought was cute.

"From mom's underwear drawer."

"You stole it!" I accused.

"No, Tammy, I borrowed it. If you wear a girdle, you can get the fat from your stomach up into your boobs' vicinity."

"She's not allowed to say *boobs*. It's a curse word."

"No, it's not. We watch the *boob tube*. What's the diff?" Elaine rationalized.

"You don't need to be thinking about tubes or boobs." Dad never liked any word that had to do with girls' bodies. Two words that would get him from a room faster than anything else were *female trouble*.

I pushed my feet up under the heater, and Elaine started reading highway signs: 42 miles to Kaladar; 31 miles to Hogue's Hollow. She read on and on, one number after another like she was a bus tour operator. I drifted off and when I came to we were at our first stop, The Cone Away from Home.

It was the same routine at every stop. He'd pull up the truck, and the owner would come out and my dad would rest his arm on the half rolled-down window and say, "Hey, Bill, (or John or Frank) what are you up to?"

Bill or John or Frank would say, "Not much."

Then Dad would say, "Well, that'll keep you out of trouble."

And they'd say, "You bet."

Then my father would put the truck in park and say, "Is it okay if I park it here?"

And Bill or John or Frank would say, "Sure, Mr. Babcock."

He'd turn off the engine and suck on his Player's Plain like he was trying to get enough breath to carry all those ice cream tubs up the steps. The lit cigarette would activate his Old Spice Cologne like an air freshener. Elaine and I always loved a man with that smell.

"You want me to help, Dad?"

"No, you keep an eye on Elaine." He knew she could talk me into anything.

Once, we were sent out to play and she told me we should put our tongues on the steel pole to see if they would stick. Hers came loose no problem, but her mother Lillian had to pour warm water on mine to get it loose. For a week my tongue tasted like liver.

People say you remember what you love about someone, but I haven't found that to be true. You remember what you hate about them a helluva lot more. I can see her standing outside the store on the sidewalk, staring off into the distance with that arrogant look on her face. Standing on one leg then switching it to the other, her girdle hooks blowing in the wind. She pushed her gut out, surveying each place like she was a building inspector.

At noon, we got the sandwiches out of the freezer. Crystals had formed on the rind of the bologna. Chew. Chew. Then dessert. We had three choices – the cheapest of course – a Nutty Cone, an Ice Cream Sandwich, or a Creamsicle. I only picked the Creamsicle once, as that orange coating was too much like fruit so once again, the ice cream sandwich won out.

Once we were done with the deliveries, we started back and that meant Dad started in on the day dreaming, sharing with us the bigger ideas he had for his life.

"You know who I think is the smartest man on earth?" he'd ask.

"John F. Kennedy," I said, knowing what he wanted to hear.

"He's the smartest in politics, but one of the smartest men on earth is Walt Disney. He doodled a mouse on a piece of paper and look where that took him."

"It took him to Disneyland." I answered right again.

"That's right."

"This year, if we get ahead of the game, we might go to Disneyland," King continued.

"We can't afford that, Dad."

"We can afford to dream, can't we?"

Actually we couldn't afford that either.

"Yeah Tammy, King and I can dream." Elaine piped in. "Would we fly, Uncle King?"

"Sure we would."

"The plane tickets alone would cost us a fortune." I didn't want him to get in any more trouble.

"Uncle King, we could drive."

"Elaine, that's brilliant."

"We could cook on the way, and it would save money – at least thirty bucks a day."

"Drive all the way to California, that's too far, Elaine, don't be stupid," I butted in.

"They're opening one up in Florida. It's going to be called Disney World. I heard it on the news," said King.

When we pulled into the driveway, Dad went into the house to talk to Boots.

Elaine turned to me and said, "There are 14 main characters in the Disney World family. Did you know that?"

"Everybody knows that." I had never heard of this.

"If we ever did get enough money to go to Disney World, you would never go."

"Why?"

"Because I know something you don't know."

"What?"

"Aunt Lillian said something. That's all."

"What?"

"Nothing."

"Whaattttttt?" She drew out the word in a long irritating whine.

"I overhead your Mom telling my mother that your family is barely getting by."

"What's 'getting by'?"

"You're broke, you moron."

"You're the broke one. We have a meat shop."

"Then how come Lillian came over last night and said she was going to have to give you away?"

"I'm her only kid. Technically that makes no sense."

"Technically it does," I shook my head, "Because you're adopted."

I could have stopped. I could have said I was kidding but then she started to cry. It was a wonderful thing, watching her face get blotchy. Her nose went first – that beautiful milky skin of hers turned red. Her girdle boobs sank back into her stomach.

She ran into the house bawling, and I thought that would be the last of it. But that's not the way karma works. I was dragged to confession for lying to her and the next week she and King went alone while I was stuck at home doing housework. When they came back that night I shot hate beams at her house, convinced I would despise her forever.

But karma is a complicated dance. That night, looking over at her place in the dusk, I saw her playing with Reg. It was hours after my Dad had dropped her off, long after we had eaten supper. She stood out there throwing the stick over and over again. With the last of the light, I saw Lillian come out of the house and she and Elaine climbed in their car to sleep.

When she slept I held her worries like a purse.

* * * * * *

Weather is odd. It rains on people's birthdays and is sunny at their funerals. The morning after Boots went mental, the sun shone like it was the most joyous day on earth. The cats sunbathed in the living room window with their bellies up to heaven.

The night before, I'd been awakened by people moving around downstairs. At first, I thought it was Nana, come for her weekly walk-about. Often she'd wander over in the middle of the night so we never locked our door. She'd let herself in and make herself hot milk with butter and pepper to calm her nerves. It was some mid-wife's potion she made that also cured sunburn and athlete's foot. But this time the noise was coming from outside. I could hear King's voice first as he whispered, "Who's out there?"

"Be careful, King." Alberta sounded mad but she was scared.

The motion light came on above the garage, and shone in my window. I looked out my bedroom window, and the brutish man stood there crying. He sounded like a cow when they take away its calf in the spring. Bleating. I pressed my nose against the pane. There was an ember. Boots and his cigarette stood in the light of the full moon. He was looking agitated, dancing on the spot like a boxer. King stepped into the pool of light. He had no shoes on and no shirt, only his pants with his skinny rack and balloon belly pooched up over his belt.

"Come on Boots. Nothing is so bad that it won't look better in the morning," King said, trying to calm him down.

Alberta ordered my father to get the lawn chair off the veranda and put her brother out in the shed until he slept it off. Boots didn't put up a fuss. He followed King like a disobedient child into the shed. I must have drifted off again but some time later; it might have been minutes or hours (time plays tricks on you in the middle of the night), lights danced on my ceiling. I looked out and there was a cop car. Two big necks got out of their vehicle, Andy of Mayberry and Barney Fyfe types, walking like they had just filled their pants. They drew their guns and pointed them at the shed. "Come out with your hands up." Nothing. No movement. No sound. The bleating cow had passed out. So they yelled again, "Mr. Stewart Cochrane, we are the Hawley Police Department. Come out with your hands up."

Eventually, Dad had to go in and wake him, and Boots came out staggering, looking confused about why they would be there for him. He talked a bunch of mumbo jumbo as they pushed him up against the car and felt up and down his body. There in the shed was the rifle. They took it and put the cuffs on him and he went limp, not fighting them one bit as they pushed him into the cruiser and drove off. Again the night was silent. I lay in my bed and watched the cows stand in the field under the moonlight.

Morning comes slowly after a night like that. At daybreak I went down to the summer kitchen, convinced that there would be a story to hear but the place was empty. The little ones were still asleep. King had gone off to his shop to meet with the men. Eventually, Alberta came in from the barn. She was downright cheerful, washing up by the sink.

When she didn't say anything I half thought I might have dreamt the whole event, but then she said, "You might as well stay home from school today and help with the fall cleaning."

Now to miss school was right up there with missing Mass. It just didn't happen, so this was big. I hated fall cleaning as much as I hated spring-cleaning, but I didn't complain that day. I wasn't going to miss any of the action.

For the next hour, I worked like a Trojan, sweeping the cobwebs off the roof of the veranda, and soon the kids got up and went out to play. Not long after, Nana huffed it over and followed my mother around the kitchen. The two of them were talking out of the sides of their mouths. Adults do this, thinking kids won't understand what they're talking about.

"What happened? What the hell did he do now?" Nana asked.

Alberta answered, "Mother, little people with big ears. Tammy, why don't you make yourself useful and take the kids outside."

I went out to the veranda with them and told them go play down by the swing. Then I started picking the dead leaves off the plants, trying to hear what was being said. The air was hot and humid. Not long afterward, Lillian and Elaine pulled up in their old jalopy. As Lillian got out of the truck Nana came out and said, "You look like the wreck of the Hesperus." Nana showed concern by commenting on your appearance.

They'd been driving around all night. Apparently they'd put nearly a hundred miles on that old jalopy. It's a wonder it didn't break down in a ditch somewhere. Elaine sat in the front seat, sound asleep. Lillian rolled down the window a crack so she wouldn't expire.

Alberta said, "Let her be. Come on in, Lillian."

They took her inside while I was told to vacuum. When they went into the good living room so I couldn't hear, I deked upstairs, lugging the canister behind me so they'd think I was working. With the vacuum left standing there running, I crept along on my hands and knees to my parents' room where there was a huge heating grate in the middle of the floor. I could see Lillian sitting on the divan. Her blonde hair had black roots. She twisted her hands into the 'here's the church, here's the steeple' position, saying his name over and over again. *Boots this, Boots that. Boots was thinking this, Boots didn't like that one little bit. Boots. Boots. Poor Boots. He didn't know what he was doing. He was not in his right mind. Not when he's like that. I don't know what I did, or what I said. Nothing happened, ...well.... he tried...to...well, we ran to the car...We didn't...but now they got him in there locked up in there, and when he gets awake this morning, when he's not in that way, he's not going to like it, and I'll get the brunt of it. Why did someone call them, eh? Why? Whoever did it shouldn't have done it. They should have just let him sleep it off. Boots doesn't do well in small spaces. He gets out of breath, gets all panicky, Boots does. Boots will be some upset. Yes sir, yes he will. Oh Boots. Boots. Boots."*

They sat there trying to come up with some explanation for why he acted the way he did. Growing up he was as smart as a whip; he'd won two public speaking contests. And he could be generous. "He brought me a Shirley Temple doll back from Paris," Alberta said, like that was proof of something.

They were searching for things to build up his character. They didn't understand how a man could be so mean and still be good with the elderly. Lillian had met him when she was working in the nursing home. He always took time to make a joke with the old ladies.

She said the first night he asked her out, they went to Aunt Lucy's to get some chicken. Fried like the Colonel's, but served on nice china with white buns and butter cut in squares. How could a man that ate fried chicken turn out the way he did?

Nana believed it was the war that changed him. Something horrific happened because he went in registered as Stewart Cochrane and came out as Boots Cochrane. Nobody ever explained where the name came from, but when he got home, it stuck. Stewart went away forever, the Stewart that had taken the pledge not to touch a drop until he was twenty-five.

He had gone a quarter of a century without a drop of liquor. He had been as dry as a twig. "Don't light a match near him," people would say. But then the first time he picked up a drink, it took him into the craziness. There was no looking back.

"Boots. Damn it, Boots. What were you thinking, Boots? Boots. Boots. Boots." They said his name over and over again.

That's what crazy does, gets you to say its name in every sentence.

* * * * * *

Lillian and Elaine stayed with us for a month. Everybody tried to get along which was not in our nature. The boys said please and thank you, and Marley kept her clothes on. Neither she nor her Barbie was seen naked for thirty days. Nana came over just as often, but went outside to smoke so she didn't upset the apple cart.

We were still in the summer kitchen acting like nothing had changed. We ate, did the dishes, then dropped to our knees and said the rosary. Lillian was Catholic, no Cochrane man married anything else. He had her praying for him by proxy but Lillian looked near death so she'd often fall asleep before we got through a decade.

Every night the phone would ring at the same time and it would be him. King would pick it up and listen to the voice, then would return it to the cradle without saying a word. I thought: Boots getting his one call from jail. I didn't understand how the cops could let him torment us the way he did but it wasn't the cops that were letting him phone. It was the nurses.

A couple days later we were playing church out near the barn, with the little kids. It was a game where Elaine appointed herself the priest and I was cast as Mary Magdalene, 'A fallen woman.' Marley didn't understand Elaine's joke, but it didn't stop her from chasing me around the chicken coop trying to knock me over. "Fall down, fallen woman," she yelled over and over again. Elaine would then bless and redeem me. Alberta interrupted us by saying she and Lillian were going into town with King.

Elaine watched the car pull out of the driveway, and

when it was clear and out of sight, she stopped the priest charade, tore off the bathrobe, then looked over at me and jerked her head like I was supposed to follow her. Marley wanted to come with us, but Elaine turned to her and said, "You can't come with us, doll."

"Why, Elaine?"

"Because if you do, you'll go to hell. You don't want that do you?"

Marley didn't cry. She thought it was funny and started talking to her naked Barbie. "Barbie doesn't want to get to hell, no sir, not hell. Not bad at all."

We could hear her babbling as we took off running towards Elaine's house. I still see myself running after her, legs scrambling through the fields of rocks and thistles, tripping over my two feet. I still have the scars on my knees. By the time we got to her place, I was bloodied and winded. Elaine opened the door to the meat shop. It was in the same place our woodshed was. I had been in the meat shop a couple of times but never in the rest of her house. Kind of odd when you think about it since we'd lived beside each other our entire lives, but we never went over to her house. Not for cards, a meal, or a visit. Nothing.

We were a clean people, but our house looked lived in. It was always full of newspapers and school projects spread around and puzzles with half the pieces missing. When we walked into her kitchen, it was just the opposite. Not a thing was out of place. It sparkled from top to toe. Everything was high gloss white. White appliances, white cupboard top, white table. No stains. No spilled food. No sign of life. If Lillian had ever cooked, there was no sign of it. I might have thought they were clean freaks until I noticed the piece of lumber under the table. An old slab of dirty hardwood put under the chair at the head of the table.

This was where Boots sat. The boss sat at the table. A piece of wood set under the chair. I didn't understand what this was for until later. Drinking so much, he'd not notice he shit himself so they put a piece of wood under where he sat so he could shit himself in peace.

Elaine ran up to her room with me following. There were no toys. Not a doll on the bed. There were no clothes lying around. In her closet there were three dresses, a couple of sweaters and pants. No summer clothes jammed on top shelves, no photo albums. Everything was on hangers, even her pyjamas. With its single bed, a white dresser, and one beige suitcase by the door, it looked like a jail cell.

As Elaine changed into some old jeans I noticed her bedroom door had no handles. There was a hole where the doorknob would have been. There were also four other holes – black holes the size of marbles that had streaked the paint. Bullet holes. "Your room is airy," I said, trying to be casual.

"Yes, well it's mine," Elaine responded.

"No. It's nice." I smiled.

She zipped up her jeans with the crease down the middle and looked at her pink watch. Then she said, "We don't have a lot of time."

As we went through the kitchen again she grabbed a few cookies and then we went back to the meat shop. "Hold up a minute. You wait here." Elaine went outside and surveyed the shop with its silver weights and saws. In a couple of minutes she returned, pulling her red wagon out of the garage.

"Are we having a parade?" I asked.

"No, a funeral."

Elaine opened the door to the walk–in meat freezer and pulled something wrapped in a wool blanket and flopped it down on top of the wagon. A bone, I assumed, to add to the reality. Then we went outside and she grabbed a shovel. We went up through the fields around to the edge of the property – the line where her life and mine were divided. As we rolled over the rocks, the object on the wagon kept falling off. We would take turns shoving it back on. There was a wooden stake where her property ended and mine began, and she rolled the wagon over onto my property.

"Now you're safe, boy."

That's all she said and then she pulled the cover back to reveal the dog, Reg. There was steam coming off him. He was stiff like lumber with his eyes staring up at the sky like he was surprised to be dead.

"My God. Who did this?" I asked.

She looked at me like I was a retard or something. "Who do you think?"

"Boots?" I asked. "Why? Did it have rabies?"

"The dog or Boots?" She started laughing like she'd just said the funniest thing ever. I continued to stare, not knowing one good reason Boots would've had for shooting a dog.

"He shot the dog?" I asked.

"Yes."

"Reg? He shot Reg? He shot Reg?"

"Yes, yes, yes."

"Why would he shoot Reg?"

Elaine explained, "I can normally tell. I know the right time to get out. She never does, but I do. Every time she acts like it's a big surprise but this time there were different variables. He didn't scratch himself. He didn't put on cologne, the Old Spice like he normally does. I left it too long. By the time we got out, well it was too late to run to the car. He was on our heels. I had to make a decision, right? To get to the car, open the door, 18 seconds. He was on us. It was too far. See? It takes thirteen seconds to run it for me. Fourteen for her and then we had to put the key in the ignition. That's one second and it takes two point five more seconds to put it in gear. He had a gun. So I made an executive decision and we ran to the shed. I should have known, but I was thinking I could run out to the field if we needed to. The dog was agitated, and he called for him. The dog ran out. I couldn't hold him and the dog ran out."

"I know but...poor Reg."

"Don't poor Reg me. Help me dig, or go the hell home."

There we were. Two figures frozen in time, digging in the backfield, with the sun was pouring down on us; kids were laughing off in the distance. We dug a few inches so that way a wild animal wouldn't dig him out. Elaine recited the phone numbers of people we knew as she shovelled. I found it comforting. Then she stood up to give the eulogy: "*Here lies Reg, twenty-two and three quarter years in people years. A flea-bitten stinking dog that rolled in cow shit and got sprayed by two skunks three months ago. Born December 14th. Died September 17th at 2:33 in the morning.*"

We covered the grave over with a mound of dirt and pointed our thumbs up in the air, singing the song from the commercial, '*Carling Red Cap, it's our favourite beer.*'

******

Nana and I were watching Hollywood Squares when out of the blue she said, "They should have locked him up and thrown away the key."

"Who, Paul Lynde?"

"No. Boots. Lillian should have done that when she had the chance. We took her down there to sign the papers. Would have given her about thirty days peace and quiet, but well... he gave her a big song and dance and well... Lillian falls for it every time."

"I thought he was in prison?"

"Prison? My God. Things haven't got that bad," Nana declared.

See, that's what my people do. When things get bad we lower our standards.

"You don't get arrested for shooting a dog," Nana said firmly, like I should have already known that. She lit two cigarettes and handed me one. We sat smoking in the dark.

ORPHANS

After the ice cream truck fiasco, Alberta decided to bake pies and sell them at market on Saturdays. She wasn't much of a cook but her recipe for piecrust is what I still use. She rendered the lard from the bacon so it would flake on your tongue. Lard snowflakes. Every Friday night we'd bake long into the night. With King, the stories were at least good and we rode around in a warm dry truck, but with her we had to stand outside in weather friendly or foul until all the pies were sold. At the end of the day, we had nothing to show for it because of some orphans in Bolivia. A priest she'd known was written up in The Catholic Register for converting small village children, apparently ever since he'd been there they were all getting stigmata. (If you say your hands bleed in this country they put you in a rubber room, but down there you get people sending cash.)

She was giving money to the orphanage, not the pies, but I thought the damn kids were getting all her best food. My pointed little head thought it wasn't fair that we never got baking like that. So when Alberta threatened me within an inch of my life, telling me if I ever touched these pies I'd be crucified, I thought 'screw it'. As soon as someone tells me not to do something I will do it. Damn the consequences. So when she was sitting there shooting the breeze with all the other farmers, I took a knife where the fork holes were and slit them open wider. Then with a straw one of the other vendors gave me, I sucked out the filling when she wasn't looking. When she cut a piece to sell it to a customer, the pie collapsed. She screamed, 'TAMMMMMMMMY.' Even though I was the only one there with her, I was surprised she knew that I did it.

"How do you know it's me? I get blamed for everything."

"Who else would it have been, Tammy?"

"I didn't do it. Honest to God. Okay it was an accident."

"What happened, Tammy? Did the pie fall on your face and you started sucking it?" She screamed. "What were you thinking?"

I was thinking she wouldn't notice.

If you were a kid in this country, you were supposed to know better. You were supposed to appreciate that the kindness given to you was a gift, not a right.

When Elaine stayed with us she didn't know the Third World rule that she was supposed to play the part of the grateful orphan. When Alberta said '*make yourself at home*,' Elaine didn't know it really meant, *'I brought you here when nobody else wanted you, so do your damn fair share and be grateful.'*

They fought from the get go. Alberta lost her voice from yelling. She expected Elaine to operate the way she'd trained us. Do as she said. No back talk. No compliments. Frankly it would have been easier on everybody if she had let Elaine go about her business. But there was nothing that burnt Alberta's ass more than seeing someone not pull his or her weight.

"Like a ram, she bucks everything I say," Alberta proclaimed.

I picked on Elaine with the best of them, but the way my

mother treated her was no fun to watch. I tried to get blamed for what she did. The day we killed the chickens was called Harvest Day. Chickens would've called it genocide. We killed 100 of them every year—enough to feed three families for the winter. We were out by the shed helping King slit their throats. A chicken doesn't give up just because its throat is spewing blood, which Elaine thought was the funniest thing ever. She began timing how long it took for them to drop - "forty-eight seconds - the damn thing took 48 seconds to die. That one only lasted 28 seconds. What the hell was that thing waiting for?"

"Elaine," Alberta screamed from down near the house. She was up to her elbows in chickens. Pouring teakettle after teakettle full of boiling water on each chicken so she could pluck the feathers out.

"Grab a chicken and come help me!"

"Go rub salt," Elaine snickered.

"What?"

"She said they need salt," I yelled, covering for her.

When the chicken finally keeled over I grabbed it and brought it down to where Alberta was standing. She waved the kettle at me. I poured the water on the chicken and plucked it and the feather points cut me to shreds. Alberta said, "That one. She's just like her father."

In my family, they don't hate you because of you. They hate you because you're like some other relative they can't stand.

******

From the time Alberta got forced into farming, she started to rely on the cows for working out her emotional issues. As long as she kept milking, she'd never need a therapist. I caught her more than once asking those cows for guidance on some worry she had. "What am I going to do with those kids?" I overheard her asking one of them. "What am I doing with my life?"

The cows were good listeners and didn't give her any lip. I think she liked them better than she liked us. One night I was bringing out the pail to milk, and I caught her singing to them. "You've Got to Kiss an Angel Good Morning'. It's a wonder the milk didn't turn because Nana neglected to pass on the musical gene. Elaine didn't know the degree to which this cow attachment existed. No one had informed her and so it was bound to go badly when she tried to milk cows. Each night as the cows came in from the fields, she sat on a bale of hay and asked questions.

"Alberta, if a calf is twenty steps ahead of a heifer and is travelling at a speed of one mile an hour, how long would it take for the heifer to catch up with its baby?"

"I don't know. Get to work, Elaine."

"Thirteen minutes."

"Grab the pail and milk."

"I'm not going to grab any cow's tit." Elaine stood with her hands on her hips.

"It's a teat, not a tit."

"Why don't you settle down and have a beer, you old bag." Needless to say, that didn't go well with Alberta. She chased Elaine around the barn with a shovel covered in manure. After being chased by a gun, did Alberta really think a shit-laden shovel was going to scare her?

The next day Elaine went to school and got off the bus at her house. Everybody acted shocked. Surprised. *After all we did for her* they said shaking their heads. What liars we were. We didn't want her any more than anyone else. That night we sat down for our evening meal. We said the grace, said pass the salt and then dropped to our knees to say our decade of Hail Marys, business as usual. Everybody in the family said we did what we could. I heard King telling the men in the shop that he didn't know what to do when she left.

"It near breaks my heart," he said. And Tom or Bill or Al

shook their heads and said, "What else could you do?"

We could have tried harder is what we could have done. We could have said you come back and we'll try to be nice. Come on Elaine. Live over here. After all the *good family* was supposed to do that. But we were hypocrites, we prayed for unfortunates. We didn't live with unfortunates.

Elaine was a hard person to get along with but if she had lived south of the equator, we'd have said, "You've been through a lot. Maybe you need a little time to adjust before we send you back to Bolivia." Two weeks after she went home, they were out sleeping in their car parked at the end of our driveway.

For four more summers, the low-grade fever bubbled beneath the surface. The infection grew and mutated. No more animals were killed in the making of that virus but it was there silent and mutating. It ate away the skin until they were no longer bodies, just apparitions. Ghosts that came at night and disappeared by morning.

RAJU

In the summer of '72, a lime green van drove into our laneway. It had flowers painted on the side and was towing a small trailer. There was a black peace sign hanging from the rear-view mirror. The long-haired driver turned out to be an uncle I hadn't met since I was a baby. A dark-skinned woman sat in the passenger seat.

Nana started hollering, "Todd! Todd! Todd!" The little kids followed suit, for no other reason than to make noise. The van drove up on the grass and began going in circles until Alberta came out of the barn, screaming: "What in the name of all that's holy are you doing to my yard?" Then she saw who it was and hollered: "Todd!"

He grinned: "I'm not Todd any more. I've changed my name to Raju."

"Uncle Jew! Uncle Jew! Uncle Jew!" the little kids screamed.

"No, Raju. It's Raju."

When he got out of his van, his hair flowed over his shoulders down his back like a Greek god. The dark-skinned woman stood beside him wearing a sari. Thus began The Summer of Raju.

Nobody could get the pronunciation right. Marley called him Ragu. King called him Chef Boyardee. When Elaine and I were in our room she'd sneeze into a Kleenex and say, "Oh I thought I had a cold," and I'd say, "Oh no, you must be suffering from a rare case of Raju."

Todd had changed his name during his journey to India to find himself. This is when he met his guru. There are so many gurus in India you can't throw a stone without hitting one. This one told him the name Todd made him a seven, which was very bad luck. He'd have to become a six if he ever expected to find a woman love him. He changed his name to Raju and shortly after that, he met Jinsa in Edmonton. She was blessed with a profound numerological equation: a four. A four and six add up to a ten which equaled love at first sight.

This kind of math made Alberta's blood boil. "What a bunch of hocus-pocus! He uses whatever he likes to justify his lack of morals. All of Todd's bad luck is of his own making. Why do you think Sharon left? I'll tell you why, because he was sleeping around with everything in a skirt. When she got herself a little extra-curricular activity, he didn't like that one iota, did he?"

For Nana, Todd's new name was no better than the old one. She didn't have any say in either one of them. He'd entered the world as a runt, nearly two months too early. Old Doc Thompson had come in the middle of the night and delivered him. The size of a pound of butter, people said. Doc took one look at him and went back home to bed, declaring he'd never make it through the night.

Then J.D. called Hester McQuaid to help out. She lived two farms over and, because of an unhappy love affair, had been considered an old maid from the time she was eighteen. She didn't go to school to become a midwife but she did get lots of practice. She had helped out with the ten Nana gave birth to.

When the doctor gave up on him, Hester took the baby and placed him in the warming oven on top of the old cooker. Every couple of hours, she gave him a few drops of rum to stimulate his heart. The next morning, Nana said she was lying there weak as a kitten and heard a squeak. She was sure a mouse had gotten into the wood box, but it was the boy lying there squeaking in Hester's arms. Nana took one look at him and said, "God must have a reason for saving him. You can name him, Hester." Todd was the only name Hester could come up with. A saint's name would've been preferred but Hester stole it from one of the pages of her romance novel. Nana thought it was horrible, but you can't renege on a deal once you've made it.

All his sisters made a fool of him, treating him like one of their doll babies, thinking everything he said or did was cute. "Look at Toddy's tiny blond hair on his forearms. Isn't that so cute?"

Nobody else in the family was treated like they were special. The most the rest of them could hope for was a life of farming and being ignored. Todd became the first one to go to university, first to get a degree, a divorce and to shack up with a woman. This kind of behavior must have worn Nana's moral indignation down because when he introduced Jinsa as his co-vivant, Nana accepted her with open arms. Nana Mary only knew the name Indian from the local reserve. She had never heard of East Indians.

Jinsa's skin was the colour of double-double coffee. A red dot was pushed down in the middle of her forehead like the thumbprint we were given on Ash Wednesday. Or those red dots used at Dollar Days at the Sell-Rite. She didn't seem bothered by our ignorance maybe because she was so spiritual or maybe because she didn't speak English very well.

Raju and Jinsa parked their trailer at the back of the property behind the apple orchard, next to where we swam.

They were out of view from the neighbours but Alberta went crazy worrying about what the McQuaids and the Hunts would be thinking.

I was strictly forbidden to go back there alone. Not that I would've had time. Alberta worked me into the ground. I wasn't allowed to sleep-in just because it was summer. Every morning as soon as Alberta slammed the screen door to go to the barn I was expected to be up. I'd roll out of my bed and drop to the floor to pray. I'd wash my face and get the kids up. I had to get them to say their prayers, make their beds and wash their faces, ears and their bums. I was their mother more than Alberta was. That summer I didn't do much milking because I had those kids to manage. I'd make them pancakes, and as they were eating I would read them a story. They'd act up and I'd spank them.

I learned to cook to make up for my awful personality. It was a vicious circle. After beating on one of them for not behaving I would bribe them not to tell. "I'll make special Chocolate Foam." I hit Patrick over the head with a frying pan for spitting at Marley, and then I had to make the pair of them four-dozen chocolate cookies. Two dozen for hurting him and two dozen for her not to tell. We never had luxury items like chocolate chips in our pantry so I'd walk across the field to Hester's to borrow some from her which she gladly gave me.

"No need to return them, Tammy, just make me some of the Waldorf salad," Hester said. I had to get Nana to lend me the marshmallows for Hester's salad. That meant I had to make Nanaimo bars for her.

Mornings were spent repenting for what I did the day before. At lunchtime, I was expected to prepare a hearty meal for those who would be haying until well after dark. Often, there would be twelve or fourteen people at the table. There were neighbours who seemed to drop by around eating time, especially if I had made Nana's chicken. Everybody on the farm agreed mine was better than hers. Because Jinsa was a vegetarian, I experimented making carrot soup. I followed the recipe faithfully but it was very plain to the taste. When they sat down to the meal, the hired help at least tried to be kind but Marley scraped it off her tongue and said it tasted like poo. Everybody laughed at that. I took away their bowls in a huff and slammed down the fried chicken on the table.

"There is no point in trying anything new on you bunch of carnivores." I didn't say this out loud of course, but I banged the pots so loudly they all hurried back to the field, all except for Jinsa who offered to stay and help me clean up. While I stood by the stove crying over the pot of soup, she came over and took a spoonful of it. She said, "That's better. All it needed was a little salt."

* * * * * *

Cooking got me out of some of the housework. If I didn't finish a chore to Alberta's liking, I could always win her over by making something special.

The real benefit was I could eavesdrop on conversations, especially the ones Nana and Alberta held daily about the occupants of the trailer. In the morning, I would make some buns and put them in the warming oven to rise. It was the same warming oven they had put Todd in, so just like him, they came out beautifully. Nana would wander over from her house or from upstairs if she had been sleeping over. She would show up around eight, pour herself a cup of coffee, and stand in the kitchen with a cigarette in one hand and the coffee in the other.

Normally, if Nana was stinking up the place with her smoke, Alberta would give her hell and bring out the Glade. Now there was a distraction: that trailer with those people back there. Alberta would take off her boots, pour a cup of the coffee that had been sitting on the woodstove since dawn, and they'd start in on avoiding the topic they wanted most to talk about. They'd talk about church and the CWL. They'd discuss good apples, the sour and delicious ones, or how the wormy apples had fallen off the trees and if they didn't gather them up there weren't going to be any left to put in the fruit cellar. On and on until something out by the trailer got their attention, something like Jinsa floating by in a flimsy gown.

"My God, is that a nightgown?" Nana would gasp. "You can see half way to China through that thing!"

"They're just managing to crawl out of the sack now? Alberta would sniff, "The day is half over!"

Jinsa could've washed in the river, but she hated the slimy stuff beneath her feet. Instead, in full view of the two gossips watching her from the summer kitchen, she would lift up the material of her sari and reach underneath to clean her privates.

"That must be the East Indian in her coming out. It's certainly not Canadian to be bathing right in broad daylight," That would be Nana. They'd shake their heads and Alberta would add: "What is that Todd thinking running around with the likes of someone like that? He's always been as odd as Paddy's Pig."

After a bit, King would come in from the shed to get a bite to eat. He spent most of that summer fixing a combine over at the Martins' Dairy Farm. He'd get one part working and then another part would go. He was such a homebody, he'd come back mid-morning for a drink of water and a nap. When he saw the two women staring at the trailer, he tried to get in on the action.

"What are the nimrods doing today? Oh, bathing. Don't they know we've got running water?"

"Looks like they're going to have lunch," Alberta said.

"What are they cooking? Squirrel?" Alberta frowned at him. "Don't look at me like that, Alberta. They're acting like hillbillies, and you know it."

"King, they're not hillbillies. They are hippies."

"Hippies? What the hell is the difference?"

"Education. They're educated people."

"Well, the educated people are camping out while we're in here using electricity and water."

"I swear King if you don't shut up, I'll brain you."

"Alberta's right, they're not hillbillies, King," said Nana. "Hillbillies don't rub your feet." That stopped the argument dead in its tracks. They turned and looked at her like she had three heads.

"They rubbed your feet?" Alberta asked.

"I went out there and brought them some cookies the other day, and Jinsa asked me if she could rub my feet."

Neither King nor Alberta knew what to do with that information. We aren't the kind of people who go around getting our feet rubbed.

Alberta was dumbfounded. "That's the strangest thing I've ever heard."

"She lit up some incense and rubbed some Patch Oil on me and I fell right to sleep," Nana continued, "It was grand."

"Oh my God, Mother, I don't believe what you are turning into."

Alberta put her boots on and went back to the barn. Dad went back to his shed to get some mid-morning shut-eye. Nana took her socks off and danced barefoot through the wet grass to the trailer.

When I finished sweeping up the kitchen floor, I walked into the orchard. I'd been told not to go there but it was too tempting. It was like the midway being in your backyard and you weren't allowed to have a ride. I pretended I needed some apples for a pie but instead, I got down on my stomach to listen to their conversation. I lay there in the wet grass hoping for a morsel of information, something to help get me through looking after the brats. I didn't hear a damn thing except for Nana oohing and ahhing a lot, saying that the ball of her foot hurt.

I didn't think anybody noticed that I was there until

Jinsa came out of the trailer and yelled, "Tammy, do you want some lunch?"

It's hard to hide in three inches of grass.

"Tammy?"

"Oh hi," I said standing up. Then I looked around and reached up to pluck an apple and waved it at her like I found what I was looking for.

"Come on over for lunch." She waved her arm in my direction.

"No thanks, I just ate." I hadn't.

"Are you sure? We've got lots."

"No thanks, I'm just picking apples. Right here under the tree."

"Okay then," she said, smiling. Todd chuckled.

Elaine joined in, relishing the joke at my expense. She hung around with them all summer. They never got a lick of privacy because she never went home. She came to our house one day and Alberta handed her a face cloth, "Boil up some water and give yourself a good washing."

"Leave me alone," Elaine yelled. "I smell because we worked out last night, doing Hatha Yoga,"

"Yoga?"

"Jinsa and Todd are Hindus, and the Hindus do Yoga."

"Todd is Catholic."

"He's Hindu now."

"He is not." To Alberta once you're a Catholic you're always a Catholic.

"He says he doesn't believe in Jesus."

"What do you mean he doesn't believe in Him? Jesus isn't Santa Claus."

"They believe in Him, they just don't worship Him," Elaine continued, "So we did Yoga, and then we cleaned out our nostrils by pouring warm salt water through them."

"Why would you do that?" I asked.

"It's a purification process. We closed off one nostril and

poured the water into the other nostril and laid our head on our side to let the water drip out."

"How did the water get into your nostril?"

"We used a small oiling can. Don't worry, I washed it before I used it."

"Did you wash it after is the real question." said Alberta.

* * * * * *

Dad was wrong about one thing. There was a big difference between hillbillies and hippies and that difference was Wacky Tabbacy. Elaine gave me the scoop up in my bedroom later that day. She'd finally taken a bath and she was drying off. She didn't mind parading around naked in front of me. She had skin you could skate across. As she sat in front of me toweling herself off, she gave me a progress report.

"Guess what?"

"What?"

"Todd lit up a dubie in front of Lillian." Elaine sat and folded her legs into a lotus position.

"Really?"

"It was breakfast time, and there they were at eight in the morning smoking a joint. Lillian had come by before work. Jinsa said to her, Hey Lillian, do you want a puff?"

"Holy crud." I asked, "What did Lillian do?"

"She smiled her smile." Then Elaine imitated her mother's voice, "Isn't it hot for this time of year? Here, I brought you some the berries fresh out of the garden."

"Did she smoke it?"

"No, but I did."

"In front of her?"

"No. She would've had an infarction."

That was Elaine's favourite word at the time. "I almost had an infarction," she would say. "My God, what's happening? Have an infarction, why don't you?"

"After Lillian left for work, I took it and smoked," said

Elaine, and then she inhaled like she was smoking and held her breath.

"Say: 'Honest to God.'"

"Honest to God."

"Honest to God?"

"Honest to God!"

"You ...smoked...up?"

"Yeah. I smoked."

"You smoked shit!"

"Pot."

"I know. I am not an idiot. So were you stoned?"

"I think so. I laughed a lot and listened to Jethro Tull."

"Jethro Tull! Oh my god. You were stoned."

"You are going to be in so much trouble," I said. I felt sick that I hadn't prevented this.

******

By mid August, they had decided to head back west. Jinsa had to finish her degree and Todd had to finish teaching her. The night before they left, they asked Alberta if we all would come down to the river for a bonfire before they hit the road.

"Fine but none of your funny business, all right Todd?"

"We'll be cool."

I expected cool would include drugs. But when we arrived at their campsite, it was so average looking, I almost expected some Girl Guides to pop out of the bushes. Todd was wearing a plaid shirt and sweat pants and drinking a Red Cap. Except for his long hair he could have been mistaken for a guy you'd see at a provincial park.

"Welcome," he said hoisting his brewski to Alberta. He hugged her longer than she felt comfortable with. He pulled out a wire hanger and showed the younger kids how to make spider wieners. He'd slice the wiener in four separate places and when it cooked it would fan out like a spider. Elaine grabbed one and gobbled it up.

Alberta looked at me and said, “It’s Friday. We don’t eat meat on Fridays in case you forgot.”

Todd winked at me as if he understood what I had to put up with then plucked a marshmallow from the bag and popped it into his mouth. There we sat, bundled up on a summer night. There wasn’t a cloud in the sky. Stars danced over the darkness. Crickets rubbed their legs together to chirp out an end of summer melody.

Jinsa told us her folks were very strict Hindus and had arranged for her to come to Canada for her education. After she finished her degree, she was supposed to go back and get married to a man her parents had chosen for her. When she met Todd it changed everything.

“We’ll just make sure you’ll never graduate,” teased Todd.

We were all holding on to every word she said, and then a strange word came out of her mouth, “Chakra.” The word blew by like smoke. Chakras, Jinsa said, are our energy centers, like an underground city linking one part of the body to the next. She wondered if we would like to open our Charkas. We all were confused by her request but being a polite people, we said: “sure.”

Nana added: “I’ll open whatever you like. Clean me out. Change the brake pads while you’re at it.”

So there we sat as Jinsa guided us through the land of Chakraville.

“Close your eyes and let us imagine the Throat Chakra which is connected to the Heart Chakra, which is connected to the Spine Chakra, which is connected to the leg Chakra. See the colours.”

Immediately I saw colour and heat swirling around me like a rainbow. The whole thing only lasted five minutes, but it seemed like forever. We opened our eyes and Jinsa was smiling.

"How does everyone feel? Relaxed?"

"I feel like a million bucks," declared Nana.

Alberta stared ahead silently into the dark night like someone had opened up the "pickle up the ass chakra." She gave King a look. He jumped up, picked up the lawn chairs and said, "Well, it's past our bedtime, folks. Come on kids, let's hit the hay." They all fell into line, but I stared ahead like a deaf woman.

"Tammy, are you coming?" asked Alberta. I said nothing.

Todd said: "It's only nine-thirty, Alberta. Let her stay awhile."

"Well she has to get up early to milk." Alberta's eyes drilled into my back.

I knew this was a test. She was thinking who are you going to choose Tammy? I stayed where I was.

"Fine then." Alberta picked up her camp chair and marched off without saying goodbye. King and the kids followed.

I was longing to do something I wanted to do for a change but I felt guilty just the same. Raju broke the silence.

"Alberta always seemed to have the weight of the world on her shoulders from the get go. I don't think she ever recovered after they sent her to St. Theresa's for high school."

"In Furlong?"

"Yes, at the convent."

"She was going to be a nun?" Elaine snorted. "God help us."

"Not a nun. JD wanted her to get a good education so he sent her there. She had to stay with the nuns because there was no way to get her home every night. So she boarded down there in the city. Only twelve years old. She did the dishes morning, noon, and night to earn her keep."

"Nana didn't want her?" I asked. I couldn't imagine Nana surviving five minutes without Alberta.

"Mother wasn't here. After I was born, she left to go to

Syracuse because her sister lived down there."

"She left you? Just up and left a baby?" I was shocked.

"She did the only thing she knew how. My mother was worn out with ten kids and she couldn't stand the thought of any more. The only solution to not getting pregnant again, was to pack up and leave. That was the only form of birth control she had."

"Who took care of you?" I asked.

"Your mother."

"Alberta?"

"J.D went and got her from the nuns. She fed and clothed and washed me, even though she was just a teenager."

"Wow."

"That's the way it was back then. But it made us tight, you know? There was some kind of heavy soul connection. I think that we were married in another life. We had to work out our karma."

"Really." I didn't know what the hell he was talking about.

"Yeah karma can be harsh, right?"

Sometime during that evening, an executive decision got made. By the next morning, I was told that they would take Elaine back with them. It would help the situation over there at the not-okay corral. She could go out west to start high school, be able to get a fresh start.

They decided to leave the trailer down by the river because they wanted to make good time getting back. The last I saw was Elaine sitting in the back of the van, dressed like Jinsa with blue sunglasses, patchouli oil and flowery skirts, going somewhere I wasn't. I hated that she was going off to some new life.

I stood in the driveway trying not to look like a knob wearing my red shorts with black Wellingtons. Elaine made the peace sign and said, "Dig it, man." They said they'd be back the following June.

Jinsa motioned me over to the window and said, “You’re very sensitive, you know.”

“Thanks.”

“It wasn’t a compliment.” She shook her head, “It’s heavy karma having an over- developed Third Eye.”

Uncle Raju gunned the engine. I stood in the driveway rubbing the space between my eyes on my forehead.

THIRD EYE

Elaine had always been a burden to me at school. We were fine when we were at the farm; when we showed calves at the 4-H barn, during the fair. We were okay when we did parades on our side road. For Christmas concerts in the living room I could manage not to kill her.

Summers and school holidays we were inseparable but when we got back to school, I would distance myself. Everybody knew that her father was a monster so they should've been kind to her. That's not how it works. The kids hated that her eyes twitched, that she had memorized all their phone numbers. The boys once tried to overturn their car because Elaine and her mother had fallen asleep in it in the school driveway. The teachers seemed to be gunning for her, too. They did that with any kid whose parent was a loser. They started treating the kid like they would be one too.

When she said, 'Tammy, you're my best friend,' I wouldn't say it back. I was waiting for another best friend to come along. Someone I hadn't met yet, someone who was equal to me.

I don't know why I thought I was so great. I was a red-blotched skinny kid who smelled like the barn. I had never made any friends, outside of my relatives. I was just a weird farm girl who made up so many stories, one teacher wrote in my autograph book: "You're so funny but I can't believe a word you say, Tammy."

Even before Elaine left, I thought Grade Nine would be my chance to re-define myself. I had planned to be popular, to spray Sun-In dye to make my hair blonder. I was going to wear lip-gloss that smelled like cherry and wear patent leather boots. It was going to be a new beginning for Tammy Babcock.

But Jinsa's parting words stayed with me. At a time when my biggest concern should've been developing a good laugh, I was in the school library scouring the Encyclopedia to find out what a third eye was and why I had one. I willed the book to tell me more about this whole thing and all of a sudden the book opened to: The Complete Works of Yogic Postures. In the back was a diagram of the chakras, and there was the definition of the Third Eye. "The second chakra, located in the middle of the forehead is called the window of clairvoyance and spiritual vision."

Two eyes help you see what is happening in the physical world. But the truth that says: 'hey I know what is going on here', that is the Third Eye speaking. Or you're paranoid delusional. It's a very fine line. A person with a strong Third Eye isn't a psychic. I couldn't predict the outcome of a horse race but I could tell if the jockey was mad at me. I could see what could've happened, and what might happen.

I knew when Alberta was about to go nuts, usually on high holidays. Any time company was coming it was certain she would blow a gasket. I knew that if I swept the cow parlour for sixteen minutes, she would make me do it again. Sixteen minutes wouldn't do. Eighteen would. So I would sweep for sixteen then I'd sit down and wait two minutes.

At school, I could see things the teachers couldn't. I

could see that Roberta Delmar was going to die a terrible death by snowmobile. (She's still alive now, but she is dating a guy from the sporting goods store so it's just a matter of time.) I knew that the goalie from the Hawley Beavers was not going to the NHL because his girlfriend Cheryl was pregnant. I had seen her puking at 4-H club. She blamed it on the smell from the hemming tape we were ironing, but I knew differently. Every time Alberta puked over basting glue, a baby came. I told Cheryl to go to the doctor.

She said they used rhythm. I wanted to say, Oh Cheryl that's how my mother had five kids.

While others wrote in autograph books, my third eye took notes. Jotted down when King was going to buy something stupid. I knew with one hundred percent accuracy that Alberta would go ape shit about it. I watched him eat cornflakes and read his motivational book, The Power of Positive Thinking by Norman Vincent Peale. I had a terrible premonition that he would die, too. There was something about the way he scraped his spoon against the cornflakes bowl to get the last of his milk.

King wouldn't let me work my Third Eye on him so I tried it on Alberta. I worked in the barn with her to show my love, worked until my hands were bleeding from ammonia and piss. I was giving off love, love, love, but her miserable energy was more honed than my positive energy. One day the Third Eye moon beamed across the hay, and I realized I wanted to stab the black-hearted bitch in the temple. I saw her in my mind, bleeding out among the Holsteins.

This is when the whole thing turned on me. I thought maybe I shouldn't be messing around with Third Eyes. It was blasphemy. Catholics weren't likely allowed to have Third Eyes. It's religious cross-pollination. It was like the Ouija board at my birthday sleepover. I had forgotten about that. Satan makes people forget. Todd and Jinsa? They were agents of the devil himself. They abandoned God. They believed in meditating and chakras, and they told Elaine to give me a hot dog.

I tried to will the Third Eye out of existence. King told me you couldn't kick people out of their apartment without sixty days notice. I figured Satan needed the same lead-time. I approached Satan like he was a tenant and I was a landlady. I began wearing my crucifix, started going to Mass in the middle of the week, like some old lady cramming for her finals. I went to confession over and over again. I went to confession so many times the priest asked me if I needed to tell him anything really bad.

When you think Satan is gunning for you, it doesn't help your REM sleep. I would wake up every night and go out into the good living room. King would often be there with a pillow between his knees trying to get the knots out of his knees.

"What are you doing roaming around?"

"I can't sleep."

"Are you lovesick?"

I have a Third Eye now and Satan possesses me.

"Pardon me?"

"Nothing," I said.

"Get back into bed with your mother." I did. I crawled in beside her and stared at her while she slept. I watched her breathe and wondered how she could not know her own daughter, not know that I could see into her tormented soul. I got close to her to see if she was still breathing and she opened one eye and said, "If you don't stop this nonsense, we are going to take you to a psychiatrist."

Instead, we did the next best thing, we went shopping. I'm sure she meant well, but it made me nervous when Marley asked if she could come along with us, and Alberta said, "Not today sweetheart, Tammy needs a little TLC."

When we waltzed into the Sears Cafeteria and she told me I could order anything I wanted on the menu, I looked around to make sure the men in white coats weren't going to come in and take me away. The last straw was when she handed me a gift wrapped in real gift paper, not newsprint. It was this bunny wrapping paper, as it was nearly Easter. No one in our family got Easter gifts. It wasn't done.

However, it did come with the normal song and dance.

"Now listen, I spent fourteen seventy-eight on your Easter present. That's why I'm taking you out for lunch because I wanted to spend twenty dollars on you. Go ahead and open it. I was very excited buying this. I would love this present for myself. Be careful, you'll tear the wrapping paper. We can re-use it."

I opened it and it was a skirt, one of those mini, midi and maxi skirts all rolled into one. You could unzip it for different lengths. It was store bought, and the first thing in my life that she hadn't sewn for me. I still have it. I'd be wearing it right this minute if I could get my fat ass into it.

"Hey cool."

"Does that mean you like it?"

"Yes," I reassured her in a calm voice.

"Well, if you don't, just say so. Don't worry; it won't hurt my feelings because I've got the receipt. Sears always takes things back. They're good that way."

"No. I like it." I did, but the more I said it the more it sounded like I didn't. It might have been a beautiful moment, in some families but in mine it was awful. We don't do love well.

"I hope it fits." She wiped her tears away. "You've lost weight. I thought you were on a diet so I got a size ten, but if you go back to normal, we'll just get a bigger one."

I took a long look at her face. The face I had been looking at for my whole life. The face I got up to stare at in the middle of the night. It was that face that I now look like, that inspired me to ask,

"Have you ever thought of wearing make-up?"

"Make-up? What in God's name for?"

"You look pale, and sallow."

"I hate makeup."

"Oh, all right. Never mind."

"No. No. I can try it, whatever you want, if that would make you happy, let's go then. We'll do me over."

My poor mother was trying so hard to drag me out of my funk. I should have let her off the hook but instead I dragged her over to the make-up counter and insisted on her being rebuilt. There we sat, two plain Jane's with this Barbie woman, with platinum hair demonstrating how my mother needed a cleaning regime if she ever expected to be happy. She reached underneath the counter and brought out a tray of sponges, scrubs, astringent and exfoliates. Then she began sanding off years of wind, sun and hard work. After every pore had been swung open, she closed them up again with a coat of foundation and blush. After an hour my mother looked wonderful. It shouldn't have mattered, seeing her look so glamorous, but it did. It was reassuring that she could be pretty, perhaps interesting.

The feeling was short-lived. By the time we backed out of the parking lot she had picked the mascara off. When she was backing up she took one look at herself in the rear view mirror and wiped the lipstick off with a Kleenex, "I look like a chicken's arse turned inside out."

* * * * * *

Two days later Elaine arrived home. She had taken a bus home from the west, a long old haul that had made her ankles swell. She had to sit in the back by the toilet so she could put her legs up.

When she got close to our place, she had the driver let her off at the four corners and hoofed it in. When I got off the school bus, she ran down our driveway to meet me. I still can feel her cold bare arms.

"I missed you. I missed you." She said it over and over

again, pulling on me like I was a wishbone. When I hugged her I could feel how heavy she had gotten. She wasn't fat by any means but she had always been on the scrawny side. When Nana came out a few minutes later, first thing out of her mouth was, "You're as big as a barn."

Elaine was the happiest I had ever seen. She couldn't quit yapping about her trip home. They had four drivers on the bus and they all had the same big belly, "Looked like they were about to deliver a kid." Alberta had to throw a wet blanket on the mood by telling Elaine she was surprised to see her before the school year was over. Without missing a beat, Elaine informed us she'd been attending an alternative school that one of Raju's professor friends had started up "It was so cool. We acted out the periodical table as cowboys."

"Sounds like a school for circus performers," Alberta said forgetting about her own singing to cows.

Elaine didn't let Alberta's negativity faze her. Instead she reached into her blue rucksack, and pulled out a report card and handed it to her. It was full of A's. Elaine kissed her on the cheek, and then announced she was taking me for a walk. It was spitting rain that was half sleet, but I guess Alberta was so shocked by Elaine being nice to her that she didn't notice and said sure. We bundled up and walked down to the creek, shivering like feral cats. Elaine piled up a bunch of wood and made a fire that spit and sputtered, more smoke than flame. She pulled out a flask of rum and handed it to me.

"The best rum in the west - Captain Morgan Black," Elaine remarked.

I took a slug of my first drink. Ever. I can still taste it. It caught in the back of my throat going down. Hot. Burning. The brain quieted. The third eye saw double. The devil took a seat at the back of the bus. I handed it back to her like I had been drinking from a paper bag my whole life.

She shook her head, "No that's for you. That shit makes me go off my head."

She pulled a "j bird" out of her coat pocket but didn't offer me any. The more buzzed she got, the more she jabbered on what it was like out there. Some days she had nothing to do because she didn't have to go to school if she had got her homework done. Raju took her to the university and she'd roam around talking to people from all over the world. People who spoke French, Chinese – even Punjabi.

"There were guys doing their Ph.D.'s in physics, actual Rocket Scientists. They were the smartest people I ever met. They talked about chaos theory versus random theory. They thought I wouldn't understand. They talked real loud to me, you know, the way city people do when they find you're from the country, like you're dense or something? I knew what the theory meant. I did. And so you know what I said? I said, "Screw you Sexists."

I don't know how talking about the random theory made them sexist, but I was thrilled to hear her talk.

"Tammy, one night this guy - he's a fellow. Not a guy, a fellow. A fellow of Mathematical Relations, a brilliant, sexy old man who was 36 maybe 37. He was so smart, he was socially retarded, you know the type? We are talking I am telling him how much I know and then he starts groping me!"

"Gross. What happened?"

"I let him."

"Oh my God."

"I was practicing."

"Did you do it?"

"Hardly. I'm not letting some old pointed head pop my cherry.

"Did you tell Raju?"

"No. I couldn't. The guy had tenure."

"What's that?"

"It means they can do what they like." She breathed in and didn't exhale for a long time.

"Oh my gawd, Elaine," I said taking another slug.

"You've been out there living and you know what've I been doing? I've been here going nuts. Nuts. I haven't slept a wink, and I got this Third Eye thing happening and am walking around all night."

"What?"

"I have a Third Eye, okay? A frigging Third Eye."

"I don't see anything."

"It's there." I pointed to the middle of my forehead.

"That's a frown. You worry too much."

"I worry because I have a third eye. It's like I am a frigging unicorn! Jinsa told me."

"Jinsa told you that?"

"Yes, and then she left and I was stuck here while you went west."

"She doesn't know anything. That one. She's a whack job. She's not as spiritual as she lets on. What is she doing with him eh? She's with that old fart, Raju. He's 41. She's 26. When he's 50, she will be 35. When she's 40, he will be 55. When he's 64, she will be 49...."

"Okay I got it. What's your point?"

"Do the math. Her teacher is her lover. So don't be putting Jinsa up on some kind of pedestal. Jinsa can piss right off with her Third Eye, garbage. A Third Eye is like Jesus. It's pinning your hopes on something you can't see. From now on, you and I are only going to believe in things we can see with our two real eyes."

Again she took a toke and breathed in deeply.

Just outside the town limits, I drank for the first time. It didn't make me feel better but I knew it would later. From the start, booze and Elaine settled everything down inside of me. The devil, the paranoia and the Third Eye shut up just like that. My skin fit for the first time in months.

BORN-AGAIN

We said the rosary after supper every night, five nights a week. I knelt at the end of the couch and stuck the Sears catalogue underneath it so I could go through the Junior Miss section while Alberta whipped through the Sorrowful Mysteries.

We were all Catholic but when Elaine was out west, her mother, Lillian, became a Born Again Catholic, which is a Catholic on caffeine. Nana called the church she went to The Born Again Sales Barn.

"They're all window shopping for Jesus," she would say.

She went with Lillian one time to check things out, under the pretense of wanting to quit smoking.

"They have catchers," Nana said, "Men who stand behind you to catch you when the Holy Spirit enters."

They had escorted Nana and her smokes up to the front of the church. When it was time to repent, some big old guy with a fake Southern accent asked, "Do you want Jesus to heal you?" Then he head-butted Nana right between the eyes, "You're saved."

"What did ya do, Nana?" I asked.

"I belted him back." Nana lit another cigarette. "Lillian got embarrassed in front of her friends but I told her in no uncertain terms that I'm not being hit by anybody, especially a fat man like that."

It seemed Lillian was too busy praying, and Boots was too busy passing out, to notice that Elaine had come home. She went from pillar to post; Launa's place and then Berle's. She was like a suitcase you'd see going round and round on a carousal. Nobody came to claim her.

By mid-May she and I took over the trailer. We got the bright idea on one of our walks. It had been sitting out there by the creek for nearly a year, rusting out; a real eye sore. Nobody else wanted to go near it. On weekends and after school we worked our tails off, fixing it up. We cleaned out all the garbage they had left. Elaine scrubbed that place until it sparkled. I made mesh curtains in the 4-H Curtain Club - purple curtains that had purple smiley faces. We complimented them with spring flowers, phlox and lilacs. During the summer we even picked purple cabbage from the garden. Deep Purple music was the only music allowed.

Elaine claimed the only bed. She had no real bedroom to go back to, so I took the fold down table. When it was completed the kids wanted to come in and play. We made a rule that they couldn't enter unless they were wearing purple. We knew they'd never enter because Alberta always dressed us in brown. When the brats ratted us out, Alberta hollered from the barn.

"Let those kids play in your fort before I crucify you."

"It is not a fort! It is our apartment."

"Let them into your dang apartment before I crucify you."

At that moment I made a commitment to get my tubes tied. The world didn't need another mother yelling at her kids, threatening crucifixion.

Driving was not a big deal for either Elaine or me. I had been driving a tractor since I was young, and Elaine had spent most of her time on the road driving for her mother. By some miracle of miracles, Alberta gave us the car about once a week to go into town and do her shopping.

We met Ben on one of our trips to town. Shortly after Elaine arrived home, he became one of her cronies - a guy who hung out in front of the pool hall. He was a Lipinski –a postal worker, who walked around town delivering mail. He also sold a little pot on the side to teenage kids: a drug dealer and postal worker. Talk about job security. She told me later she'd met him with Raju. He had come out to the trailer to provide a few treats for them all.

Ben supported many causes. Maybe it was because Ben was Russian, but he hated the idea of any minorities being dumped on. In fact, he had been suspended from school many times defending people for absolutely no good reason: The Women's Rights Group, The People Who Wouldn't Sit by the Ugly Kids. His mind was full of ideas that were impossible to understand. When we met him, he was going through his Buckminster Fuller phase. Fuller looked up every word he used to make sure he knew the real meaning of what he was saying. Ben challenged himself to do the same thing. On the door of our trailer hung a list he created, of all the phrases we should never let ourselves say anymore: Twenty-four seven; Night and Day; Actually; Unthaw; Fill-um (instead of film).

Many nights he'd walk all the way from town to our trailer and give us lectures on his various causes.

That summer I'd been relieved of kitchen duty. Instead, I worked out in the fields until dark. There was a lot of rain that summer so we'd cut and bail the hay but couldn't put it in the barn wet so we had to wait for it to dry out in the fields. It had to be properly dried so it wouldn't mold or combust, then stacked properly.

On overcast days I would get a break by mid-afternoon.

I'd head back to the trailer and crawl into bed for a good purr. I had moved myself out there one paper bag at a time.

Elaine would just be getting up. I'd entice her out of bed with a cup of coffee and a piece of my lemon pie. Then we'd jack up the volume on our eight track. We took to calling ourselves Raju and Chef.

"Hey Raju, whatcha doing?" I'd say.

"Nothing Chef, I'm just about to have a smoke." Elaine didn't smoke real cigarettes - just the pot that Ben brought out after dark. After they'd smoke up, he'd lie back on the bed with his arms behind his head and say, "Come here, my two girls." The three of us lay there in that wonderful world between sleep and wakefulness. We'd share our dreams with each other - the stuff you would never tell a guidance counselor: who we wanted to be and what we thought about things. I wanted to be a world-renowned chef. I loved food, would talk about it in such great detail, they would inevitably got the munchies. I'd offer to go in and make grilled cheese and pickles. One night, Ben wanted us to order a pizza. Elaine pulled on her sweats and said, "We can order from my place."

"Let's not Elaine," I wanted to stay put.

But Elaine wasn't listening. She got up and started running across the field. Ben and I followed her. The full moon lit up the field as we serpentined among the cattle. When we got inside the meat shop door, she told us to stay put, as she went in to call Papa's Restaurant. We stood beside the scales and the hooks. A slab of beef hung in the freezer and the saws were there ready to cut.

The door from the shop to the house was open and I spotted Boots passed out on the couch in front of the TV which was showing the eleven o'clock news. If you didn't see the bloated face and the bottle of rye on the coffee table, he looked like a normal Dad who had fallen asleep. Then it hit me. The smell. There, in the kitchen, underneath the table where they ate, was that same board I saw the first time I visited. On it was a pool of piss and shit. When you're too busy drinking to get up and go to the can people had to put out a one stop-shopping mat, The Welcome to Poo on Yourself Mat. Lillian was the cleanest person you ever met so Crazy is like the limbo - you keep lowering the bar. There was a trail of brown shit from the kitchen to the living room. I had to get Ben out of there.

"Let's go." I pulled at his sleeve.

"Cool."

It was like there was a gymnast doing flips in my stomach. I dragged him out behind the house and he lit up another joint as he leant against the shed.

"Relax Tammy."

"I am relaxed. Thanks." I tried to look calm.

Ben took another toke and held it deeply, then took my mouth and exhaled into it. He stared at me then he leaned in and there out by the shed, Ben kissed me slowly and softly, then he moved his tongue around in my mouth like I was a butterscotch ripple ice cream cone. Before that night, I had never kissed anybody but my Dad, but there I was, kissing Ben at the back near the same shed Elaine and Aunt Lillian had hidden behind when their lives were on the line. Fear and erotica was the thumbprint. He and I pushed our clothed groins together, blue jean against blue jean until the sound of her harpy voice broke the mood.

"Billy Weiss went mental when I said I wanted it delivered up the third concession."

Elaine cut us apart like scissors. "What the hell are you two doing?"

"Keep your voice down," I pleaded. If she woke up the beast inside, we'd be dead.

Elaine continued in a loud dramatic whisper, "Just look for the sirens by the rock, that's what I said. Isn't that HEEEE larious? Billy said he didn't need any horn blaring; he just needed an address."

Elaine had given him the fire number for the Everett's place because if he'd turned in our driveway, our dogs would have barked their fool heads off. The Everett dogs barked just as much as ours did, but their parents were dead. They lived with an older brother who was a pig farmer and went to bed early. Ben hid in the bushes to protect us in case a mad killer happened to drive by before the pizza arrived.

When Billy pulled up in the delivery van, we'd forgotten one important detail. We didn't have money to pay him. Billy said he couldn't leave the pizza without any money. Ben came out from behind the bushes and gave him a small envelope.

******

Nana wanted to know what we were up to, so she made every excuse to tramp down to our trailer.

"Yoo-hoo. Anybody home?" she'd say, opening the door.

"Who is it?" Elaine asked, knowing it would annoy her.

"I've got something for you girls."

"Nana, leave us alone."

"You shouldn't be sleeping in the middle of the day. I've got something for you, a pamphlet." She unfolded it and laid it on the table. "This explains the male members of the family." She touched the pages slowly as she leafed through it, and turned right to the page where the men's body parts were laid out in Technicolor.

"Who's this member, Nana? Dick?" Elaine asked. The joke went right over her head.

"No. Medically speaking, it's called the do dad."

"I thought it was called the penis," Elaine said.

"Well, some crass people say that, but I do want you to know one thing - it grows."

"Grows?"

"Like a weed!" said Nana.

"Look we know about this stuff, Nana. Thank you," I said.

"Well, you better not know anything about it! Don't look at it until you walk down that aisle and say 'I do'."

Elaine, who had been lying on the bed, sat up and pulled her legs up to her chest.

"Why Nana?"

"Because if you saw what it did, well you'd rethink the whole thing."

"Really, Nana?"

"Absolutely. It doubles in size, swells up like a bee sting to a horrible purple colour."

"Well, that's just delicious, Nana. To think it would turn to that magnificent colour is more than I can hope for," Elaine said.

"It's sad that you both know so much about life," Nana remarked.

"What's really sad is an old woman trying to act like a young one," Elaine laughed and Nana Mary huffed out, slamming the door.

Nana's vivid description of the mail member was intended as a deterrent, but it painted a picture inside me that led to all sorts of imaginings. The next time Billy came out with a fully dressed pizza, I rubbed my foot outside the top of his crotch. The purple monster bulged beneath. Ben may have got us extra pizza, but I got it with extra cheese.

DRAMATIC EXIT

Chan and Dolly Lee owned the China Doll restaurant. As kids we had only been in there after church as a reward for our not killing each other during Mass. Chan's other job was that he was the head catcher at the Born Again Barn. As such, he had to ensure he recruited other catchers who had strong arms with good backs because there is a high proportion of Born Again's with weight problems. Most people pray to get rid of their lust when apparently they should be praying to be rid of gluttony.

Chan told me he wanted to feed Lillian from the first time she fell back into his arms. She was so light, he was convinced he had broken her ribs. Chan didn't know the gory details when he met her, but he could tell a heavy load burdened Lillian. He asked the prayer group if they could create a prayer circle for their sister. Without a yes or no, she let them form a circle around her. She lay in the middle, rocking back and forth in the fetal position, as they chanted in tongues for over an hour. She soaked it up until the stroke of eleven, when she stood up out of her trance and said she better get home because Boots would be some upset.

The prayer must have planted a seed in her, because within a couple of months she had left him. You'd think it would have been the pile of violent acts that prompted her but it turned out to be an orange peel that tipped life on its axis. She got up one morning and remembered her mother peeling a navel orange and making curlicue rings out of the rind. Delicately she placed it beside the two eggs easy over. He stumbled to the table, took one look at it, and threw the whole thing against the wall. As the yolk dripped down the wall in slow motion, she could feel the scales fall from her eyes. She walked over to Boots who was lying on the couch and said, "I didn't put an orange peeling on your plate to tick you off. I just wanted a little color."

Boots didn't hear her of course because he was passed out. Even filled with the Holy Spirit, she wasn't stupid enough to say that if he'd been conscious. What was surprising was how nobody on our side of the fence knew this was about to happen until a posse of Buicks drove up, windows down, radios playing ' The 'Old Rugged Cross'. Lillian was expecting only Chan and Dolly but Chan brought a herd of catchers with him, who got out of their vehicles, and held their hands up to the sky, waving them back and forth. One of the catchers was a cop packing a pistol. Even Jesus needs back up.

Lillian had told Elaine to wait in town but, of course, she didn't. Parents expect you to miss the most interesting parts of life. Elaine sat in the middle of the action, smoking a candy cigarette, watching men she didn't know pack up their belongings.

Boots stood with one arm on the meat freezer, squinting at the gathering of odd balls on his front lawn. He covered one of his eyes as if he was trying to bring the whole picture into focus. He watched as Elaine stole the keys for his truck. He did nothing as she burnt rubber out of the driveway. People said it took him nearly a week to twig to the fact that nobody was bringing that truck back.

Chan let them move into the apartment above the restaurant. It was a dive, about a third of the size of living space they were used to with no land, not even a back yard. But it was a safe place to be. With lots of people around, Boots wouldn't dare cause trouble. Looking out their living room window, they could see all the comings and goings of the Hawley traffic. During the day, the shoppers were right on their doorstep. They could almost tell what people had in their grocery bags.

At night, it was grand central station. For the first few times I stayed there, I never got a wink of sleep. People would come out of the bar right next door and stagger into the China Doll to order up a feed of something to soak up the booze. Sometimes we'd hear Chan running down the street after one of the dine and dashes. There was so much energy; outside and in.

Lillian had set up her bed at the end of the living room. She created her own space by cordoning it off with a silk privacy screen that Dolly had given to her as a welcome-to-your-new-home gift. We were getting ready to hit the sack one night when Lillian informed us she might be overtaken by the Holy Spirit and not to worry any if we heard her speaking in tongues.

"It might sound like gibberish, she said, "But please don't interrupt if the Holy Spirit is entering me."

I wasn't going to go near her if I heard that going on. That night I had a hard time sleeping, worrying about what would happen if Lillian conjured up the wrong spirit. Our bedroom was at the end of the hall, so I cranked up the music so I could drown her out. Our room had no windows, which was just perfect for Elaine because she was a nighthawk who loved to sleep all day.

I say "our" room because I felt like I had moved at the same time. I was still officially living at home, but my prayer face had convinced Alberta that I should be allowed to stay in town with them at least once a week. I still had to get my chores done but if I finished by Saturday night I got to stay over. So one bag at a time, I brought my stuff.

The apartment was shipshape from the moment they moved in. They didn't have any money to speak of yet they bought tons of cleaning products. Furniture was at a bare minimum. There were a few chairs and a table from the church people as well as some donated kitchen items an old parishioner had conveniently died the month before. She was a clothes horse, her family didn't know what to do with all the dresses and hats and shoes she had not taken out of the packages, so they were passed on to Lillian. In the box, there were shirts and pants all the same colour; same size. My God, there were eighteen pair of shoes. Lillian likely hadn't had a new pair of shoes since she got married. It should've made her happy to have something to step out in, but that many choices seemed to confuse her. She would stand in front of the closet door hemming and hawing, asking Elaine to tell her which ones to pick. This was the closest I had ever been to the two of them. They didn't act like mother and daughter. They were way too polite.

"What would you like to do now sweetheart?" Lillian would ask.

"I don't know mommy; what do you want to do?" Elaine responded like a small girl.

It is unnatural to get along with your mother like that. The only thing more unnatural was watching them eat. Lillian would burn some meat up beyond recognition, add a few tortured peas and that was supper. Grace went on so long, the supper got cold. Lillian had to bless half the universe and people in countries I've never heard of. I hoped the children of Bolivia are happy.

I eat fast. It's a result of being from a big family. If you hesitate, you lose out. I tried to match my pace to theirs, but I couldn't make a forkful of peas last as long as they did.

After the night time meal, the three of us would sit on the battered love seat. They had no TV so we sat there doing nothing. Saturday nights were like Tuesdays. Nothing ever happens on a Tuesday. The saving grace was board games, which are called that for a reason. I was bored. Until I stayed with them, I don't think I ever finished a Monopoly game in my life. At our house it usually ended with somebody storming off after they knocked over the table. The two of them played to the bitter end. They could do it for hours, buying Boardwalk, losing Boardwalk. Their commitment to boredom had energy to it. They were waiting for the other Boot to drop.

But it never did. The Boots who would have come looking for them was disappearing quickly, drifting off into a sea of booze. He lay around all day only getting up to freshen his rye. He was saturated with it, so it took less and less to get him to pass out. He lay there like a big hunk of decaying liver, saying the rosary.

* * * * * *

When Lillian left Boots, the family launched a campaign to get them back together. They called the apartment and invited her for lunch. Lillian walked into it and was blindsided. For years they had told her to leave him so she didn't know what hit her. They sat there espousing the sanctity of marriage, emphasizing the sickness and health part of the vows.

"It's awful to give up on a man," said Alberta.

Nana continued, "You left. You made your point. Now go back and sock it to him. He shouldn't be let off the hook that easy." For Nana, a marriage vow is not so much a promise, as a death threat.

Lillian retold the story about scales falling from her eyes, hoping that would convince them she'd been given a sign. Alberta wasn't buying it. She had a bee in her bonnet because, since Lillian left, the meat hung in the freezer: uncut, unpacked, and undelivered. Boots was going to lose everything; his shop, his livelihood, and his early inheritance. This upset JD to no end. He didn't care that his son was dying. Probably some part of him hoped for an end it all. This would put a finish to the looks in town; an end to the shame.

He was most worried that he was about to lose the shop he had financed. He complained constantly to Alberta: "You have to do something. You can't let my hard work be flushed down the toilet." So Alberta and Nana would go over after work and cut up meat, call the customers, and deliver it to them but they couldn't keep up that pace forever.

In the restaurant, talking to Lillian about love and God, Alberta told Lillian, "Sometimes we have our crosses to bear."

"From where I'm sitting, you haven't got much of a cross. You always had a good man."

"You always say that, Lillian. Look, you have no idea what my man's like. That man of mine is no flipping saint," Alberta replied angrily.

"Well he's not bad," Lillian protested.

"What goes on behind closed doors isn't always pretty," Nana chimed in. "Not pretty at all

Lillian stood up. "I've had an epiphany." I'm not going back ever."

Nana yelled after her, "I've already bought your 20th year anniversary card."

Lillian marched up the stairs to the apartment to have a shower. When she came out of the bathroom she'd done her hair up in the most pleasing way. She went to the closet and put on a pair of the new shoes. In fact every day for the next week, she wore a different pair. They put a spring in her step. She walked to and from work, saying hello to people on the street that she hadn't talked to in years. As we sat eating her burnt supper she'd say, "It's time for Lillian to say Lillian is worth something."

PIG

Elaine's one attempt at having a legitimate job lasted about ten minutes. It was during that brief honeymoon phase when they were trying to have matching mother daughter careers, that she tried working at the nursing home. But, she hated old people. "I detest the old, Tammy. Nobody that wrinkled should be allowed to exist."

The only reason Elaine accepted the job at Green Acres Nursing Home was because she thought she'd get to wear a candy striper uniform; that she'd be some sex symbol in a pink striped shirt who might be able to pick up some nice medical student. When they told her that she'd be working in housekeeping and have to wear green boxy scrubs while cleaning bed pans, she quit.

Elaine decided she was going to become a professional drug dealer. That's not a career choice guidance counselors give as an option, but Elaine put this plan into action as deliberately as any profession she could've chosen. "You can't smoke shit if you want to sell shit," is what a chorus of singers could have sung for her radio commercial. She stopped smoking cold turkey. This confused Ben. It confuses all drug users. Why would anyone not want to sample what they're selling? If you don't use there is more money; that was her theory. Elaine loved making money. She stopped smoking and started selling hash instead of pot so her profits would be higher.

There was lots of math required, which is what she did well. Elaine could keep figures running in her head like she was a giant calculator. She'd add up and subtract profit margins until my head was spinning. Some nights I'd actually be relieved to see Lillian come home so we wouldn't have to talk any more about it.

She'd ask us what we'd been up to while she was at work and I wanted to scream, "Math! Lillian, all we've been doing is math."

Lillian lived in some kind of dream world. She believed whatever Elaine said or did and never questioned where Elaine's money was coming from. Once she was far enough away from working with the old folks, she started being extra nice to her mother. Lillian ate it up. Elaine bought flowers, and massaged her feet like Jinsa had taught her. Lillian groaned with pleasure when Elaine would take off her shoes and rub her mother's tired swollen feet. After she'd have a good soak, she'd say, "Gosh, doesn't it smell good in here?" She was smelling the egg rolls and sweet and sour sauce through the vents coming up from the restaurant.

"So, why don't we go down?" said Elaine.

"Really?" asked Lillian. "We can't afford that."

Elaine pulled out a wad of twenties. Lillian looked at her, like she was about to receive her allowance. If I had done this in my family, there would have been questions. Somebody would have said 'you don't have a job. Where the hell did you get the money, Tammy?' Lillian looked at the cash and gave us one of her *ain't Jesus grand in all of his abundance* smirks. Down we went to the China Doll.

The place was hopping with the late night barflies; people sitting in a haze of their own smoke; cartoon characters with clouds above their heads. A thick layer of sesame oil grime covered the wood paneled walls. At the front entrance was a fish tank about the size of a booth, which Chan had stocked with oversized goldfish. The water was green and dingy, with fish like mud cats you would see in the crick, bottom feeders with old man eyes.

One night after everybody had gone home and Dolly had gone to bed, Chan came over to our booth. It must have been way after two in the morning so we were about leave. "Sit down. Sit down. Don't go anywhere," he said. "I have a very special treat for you."

Within minutes, out he came with a tray of silver pots and bamboo baskets of food prepared especially for us. The kind of food people didn't usually order. When we opened the lids, steam belched out of them. Before us sat a feast of fried duck legs, chicken and Broccoli with Oyster Sauce, and deep-fried Eel. Hot Pots they were called.

Lillian and Elaine weren't fussy about any of it. Egg rolls were as far as their taste buds would venture. Ben and I dove in. My mouth felt like it had been born in Beijing. The taste was clean, not heavy like meat and potatoes. I sucked the marrow from each duck leg. As I was licking sesame oil off my fingers, Chan came in from the back with a bag full of quarters for the jukebox - soon music blared, good old rock and roll. We all got our second wind. Elaine and I did some dancing. Ben tried to dragged Lillian out of the booth but she swayed back and forth with her eyes closed as Chan stared at her, humming "Stairway to Heaven".

******

Chan had a habit of throwing his leftovers in the back alley. One night, he pitched out the carcass of a barbecued pig. He didn't bag it up properly, and a cat got into it and tore at the bag until it was spread all over the back. The garbage men wouldn't take it away and Chan wouldn't re-bag it. "They garbage men, they should do garbage." It became a contest to see who would blink first. The pig sat out there for two weeks. The longer it sat, the greener it got, not a pleasant forest green, but a bright fluorescent green.

We went the back way to the apartment through that alleyway, and we would see the pig there. We tried our best not to look but a fluorescent green piece of decaying meat is hard to ignore. No matter how many times we saw it lying there, we screamed girly screams like it was the first time. Whenever anyone came into the restaurant by the back way, we could tell by the look on their faces they had seen it too.

One Saturday night, when we had just finished our feast, there was a huge crash in the alley. Bang. Bang. Lillian sat up on high alert. She ran around in circles and tried to run up to the apartment. Elaine grabbed her and told her to shush. "Stay put." Ben looked at the back door and in his best gay voice said, "No, no. It's the dreaded pig."

There was more crashing and ramming around. Chan picked up a cleaver and kicked the door open. There stood Boots rooting around in the garbage; a pig amidst the porcine.

He staggered toward Lillian, but Chan blocked his way, saying: "You get home."

Boots mumbled: "Goodbye Lillian, the good times are over."

Chan's accent came back full force, "Good times never started." He then slammed the door, dead bolting it to end the debate. We sat there not moving. Chan ordered us to bed then he ran around turning off all the lights, and we were left to feel our way to the exit sign.

When we passed the front window, we could see Boots standing in the middle of the street, teetering back and forth. He looked up and down the empty town as if he expected Superman to appear on the streets of Hawley. We heard a terrible screeching sound from far off. When it came into view it was the old Ice Cream truck, oil was dribbling from the back end. When it belched to a stop, the driver leaned over and opened the passenger door. Boots climbed in. He and King drove off into the night.

CADILLAC TAVERN

When my mother and her sisters were teenagers, their independence was doled out slowly. Their big entertainment was going to the Beaver Lake Pavilion on a Saturday night, double entendre not intended. The pavilion was a dance hall, eight miles down the road from the farm. As soon as you turned down the road you could hear the throbbing pulse of the music. The sound echoed for miles across the water. Two-step country bands played weekly, banging out all the cover hits - Elvis, George Jones, and Charley Pride. Alberta and her sisters got dolled up and drove in their old Chevy to the dance.

When she first started dating King, Alberta took him out there but soon learned he didn't have an ounce of rhythm. He didn't dance so much as bounce up and down like he was trying to pump water. Alberta put him out of his misery and let him stay outside to shoot the breeze with all the other young farmers. Even after they were married, she let him stand outside with those men from church. They'd spend most of the night drinking. The Pavilion didn't have a liquor license so they hid their stash in the trunks of their cars.

Their partner's inability to keep time had little or no effect on my mother and her sisters. I think it made it easier for them. They never sat down. When they were young, Nana used to clear away the kitchen table to teach them basic dance steps; the waltz: the jive.

Launa was the designated girl, being the smallest and the prettiest. Berle and Alberta maneuvered her around the floor taking turns throwing her between their legs and over their shoulders. Alberta said people would form a circle around them to watch their dance moves. Those Cochrane girls were an intimidating lot. If a man did get up the nerve to ask one of them, Launa was the one who said yes, partly because Berle and my mom were already taken and partly because Launa was the only one who didn't try to lead.

At midnight, they played Kiss an Angel Good Morning, then the band quit and lunch was served. There were some nicely cut sandwiches, pickles, and cheese. Old cheddar was the best. Even for dessert you could lay a slice on top of a nut square.

The tradition of a nighttime lunch was something that was dropped by the time I got out on my own. Dropping the lunch contributed to the terrible demise of my generation. The lunch put a cap on the event and ended the night in a special way. The men would come in, even the drunkest of them knew the value of eating something. Then my father would get up for a final slow turn around the room. It wasn't dancing as much as a way to connect with my mother. His knee slid between her legs, trying to oil the engine for what would go on later. Staying up late was going to mean they were tired, but farming was never going to give them a day off so they might as well have one good night a week when they enjoyed themselves.

The pavilion had burnt down before I came of age so I didn't dance. I went straight to the bars. The Cadillac Tavern was where it all began and ended. The bar was dark, except for the red Bud Beer sign over the mirror. A tacky Royal Dolton image of a fairy queen riding a seahorse posed on the shelf behind the bar. I stared at it for hours, hoping I could ride away on it.

There were only three rules in the Cadillac Tavern: you had to have a nickname, you had to wear flood pants and you had to play darts. My nickname was 'Tammy Pajama.' I wanted to be 'Tamara the Sahara,' but try as I might to insist on that name, it didn't fly which brings up rule number four: you can't control the nickname people give you.

After a couple of Saturday nights, I began to fit in pretty well, but Elaine made the regulars nervous.

Most of the old farts treated me like I was their daughter. No matter how drunk they got, they didn't try anything, not unless invited. They knew my family. Who didn't? If you threw a stone in town you'd hit one of us.

Blacky did step out of line - he grabbed one of my tits, but the next day he said he was sorry. He used the excuse, "I didn't see your breasts sitting there." After I heard him singing Tiny Boobies under his breath. He'd try to feel you up, and then afterwards buy you a pickled egg. Pickled eggs taste like ass.

It became a regular routine, our going in there on Saturday nights. We were on our own because Lillian and Dolly had started going to prayer meetings every week. Normally they'd get back late, but this one Saturday they went on a road trip to hear a preacher who had a real gift for testifying. It was too far to drive there and back in one day so they rented a motel room. This meant we could stay out as late as we wanted.

Elaine and I were sitting at the bar having a beer when a pack of hockey players walked in. It was the first and only time people our own age ever darkened the door of that place. Believe it when I say there wasn't an ugly one in the bunch. Our tongues practically hung out of our mouths. Elaine found out they were student players from Sweden, from a billeted at the homes of the Hawley Beavers.

We were average looking girls to the guys in Hawley, but to these Swedish guys, we were hot.

I tell myself it doesn't matter what a man looks like as long as he's sensitive and charming and spiritual, but it's something I say in case I get stuck with an ugly guy. The cutest Swede was off the Richter scale of blonde. He was so pale you could go snow blind looking at him. His name was Otto. All these years later, I can say his name and feel the heat of his breath on my neck. By the end of the night, he had asked me to come to the game on Friday night. He wasn't playing because he had punched out our goalie and was benched for the rest of the series.

Despite all my desperate attempts to find inappropriate love, I'd never slept with one of the losers on the local hockey team but I did sleep with Otto because he was from out of town. I went to the game. Elaine and Ben stayed up in the heated section passing envelopes to people but I made my way down to a seat behind the penalty box. I passed him a bottle of Orange Crush, spiked with vodka. It wasn't like he was going to be drinking and high sticking. By the end of the second period, the buzzer rang for intermission. Otto jumped up into the stands. He grabbed my hand and we took off out the rear exit of the arena, out to the open fairgrounds, sliding along the rock and snow. We entered the grandstand, and climbed down between the benches. My heart was pounding through my bra as he felt around at the top of my sweater, then cupped his hand over my crotch. Then he unzipped my pants. There was touching, grabbing, and groping. We pushed everything scary to the other side of the world. He unzipped his pants, and pushed my hand inside to feel his penis. It grew in my hand, like the sea-monkeys I once ordered from the back of a comic book. I pushed him down in the seat and lifted his legs onto my shoulder. I aimed his basket toward the street lamp in the parking lot. He must have thought I was experienced, but honestly I had to see what color it would turn. It was much less majestic than I had imagined. It was not purple like Nana had warned me about. I imagined lavender or perhaps a nice lilac. And then he pushed it inside of me and popped my cherry. I don't know how to be romantic about it. It wasn't romantic, but it was fast.

Elaine was pissed at me but I was glad to get it over with. I called it opportunity presenting itself. Besides if I had been bad at sex, he was leaving the country. He couldn't tell anybody I knew. Also, I had protection. Earlier in the winter, I'd had an inner ear infection and went to see our family doctor, Dr. Burkett. When he was looking in my ear with his little mirror do-dad, he asked me if I was sexually active and I said yes. At the time I wasn't, but I thought 'better safe than sorry'. He didn't sweat it, just wrote me a prescription with ten repeats, no questions asked.

Sex was no big deal. We did it so fast we got back to the arena before the third period started. Ben and Elaine hadn't moved. They were still sitting there talking to their stoned cronies.

Otto was only in Canada for three weeks so we didn't waste time. We did it more times than you could count. Elaine made me count it though. Add it up. Thirty-two times in three weeks, which was pretty good, considering there were two out of town games I was not allowed to go to. The first eighteen times were nothing to write home about. He fumbled around, not really having a clue about my body or his. But on the nineteenth time, I started moaning. I wasn't excited enough to moan, but I read in a 'True Confessions' magazine that if you moaned, it helped. When I did, Otto started to get very creative, and soon my fake moaning became real moaning.

In all the thirty-two times, he never saw how bad my skin was. It was night, and we usually did it under the bleachers or at the back of the bus; but one time we went to the house where he was billeted, and we did it in his bed. There was a light coming in from the street so I lay on my stomach, as my back was clear and smooth, so he wouldn't see any spots. He wrote messages with his fingers on my back, messages that must have been in Swedish because I didn't understand what he was trying to scribe. I moaned and gurgled, and when he tried to turn me over to look into my eyes, I turned off the light. In all thirty-two times, he didn't see the red spots on my skin or the flakes in my scalp. It gave me great hope that one day it would be possible to get married and never have my husband see me naked.

It was time for him to go. The team had to catch a bus to the airport at two in the morning. We did it three times that night - hat trick. It was like we were trying to squeeze every last bit of loving in before we were separated for eternity.

******

After Otto left, all I wanted to do was climb into bed at the apartment and sleep, but sleeping would have made it worse as it was already four o'clock in the morning and I was expected to be home to do the milking by six. After Lillian refused to come back to the farm, Alberta had been in a speed wobble. The entire burden of both farms and the meat shop had fallen to her. I should've had some sympathy for her, but I was bursting with moral indignation, that her work had become mine. I didn't ask for extra. At the same time I knew if I had called in sick, she would've come and got me.

I showered the sex smell off of me, trying not to wake Elaine or Lillian. It had snowed all night and nobody had ploughed the back roads to our farm so it took all the concentration I could muster to keep the jalopy on the road. The steering wheel pulled on the gravel, and I almost ended up in the ditch more than once. My skull felt like it was going to crack open.

When I walked in the house, the wood stove was

chugging away. King had piled on so many logs, it was a wonder the place hadn't burnt down. He was curled up on the couch with his butt facing the heat. There is a point in every kid's life where you find out your parents aren't right in the head. It's a natural thing, otherwise we'd never cut the apron strings and move on. But I hadn't planned for him to fall off the pedestal that day. When I saw his butt pointed at the fire, I hated him. Hated the man he was, always working at things that never helped anybody, never got any of us off the hook. I looked at him and realized I was smarter than him, and funnier. I also realized he was the kind of man who could never tolerate anyone telling stories better than he did.

All my life he said think for yourself but what he really meant was think like me.

I had been on my way to these realizations ever since I got my first bra. I hit 13 and my Dad stopped making eye contact, as if looking at me would turn me to stone. Once you ovulate you start feeling like you're doing something wrong. You spend the next ten years getting your father to look you in the face again.

My mind was swirling with these thoughts, when Alberta came down and started in on me.

"Why are you wearing sunglasses?" she asked.

"Because your beauty is blinding me," I said sarcastically.

"Don't be lipping me. You have a bruise on your neck."

"I got hit with a puck."

"Get to the barn, Tam," King spoke from his slumber. He stretched out, moving into a yawn that sounded like a rusty door. The sound infuriated me.

"Why don't you?" I mumbled it half under my breath. Part of me hoped he hadn't heard, but I couldn't take it back.

"What did you say, Tammy?" Alberta stopped in the middle of pulling on her Wellingtons.

"Nothing."

"Come on, let's get." Alberta tried to hand me my overalls, but I ignored her and continued to give King the evil eye.

"I have one question. Do Swedish men let their women do all the work?"

"What?" King pulled on his filthy wool socks; his toenails looked like a vultures' beaks.

"I'm just wondering if men in Sweden sit around all the time letting the women do their work."

"How the hell would I know? I've never been to Sweden," said King.

"That's right. You've never been to Sweden, or Florida or Disney World.

"God you've been nowhere, King." I stood over him.

"Don't talk to your father that way." Alberta was getting flustered.

"Swedish men don't get their wives to do their work for them."

"What has Sweden got to do with anything?" Alberta didn't know what I was talking about.

"In Sweden, they are open-minded and liberal."

"Stop your nonsense," said Alberta and pushed the overalls at me.

"I'm not going." I looked intently at her.

"What?"

"I'm not going out there to do his work. I am not going to milk cows ever again."

"What?" Alberta couldn't believe what I had just said.

"Jesus, Tammy," King piped in.

"You get to hate cows, Dad. Well so can I. I'm not going to that goddamned barn ever again."

Alberta didn't say a thing and then out of nowhere she began pounding on me like she had done a hundred times before. He sat and watched as if there wasn't a damn thing he could do about it.

When I was little, I used to go somewhere else; fly above it all. I'd let myself float up to the ceiling somewhere where I couldn't feel the pain but that day I had just been touched in a nice way for hours. My legs were shaking from someone loving me so when she belted me, I grabbed her wrists and twisted them like you do when you wring the neck of a chicken.

"Don't you ever hit me again," I said.

"King, do something." Alberta screamed.

"You two stop it. Why can't you get along with your mother?" he said sitting up like he might do something but he didn't. "Get along."

I said, "No more listening to you criticize everything I do. No more you. No more farming."

"What in God's name are you talking about?" Alberta cried out.

I dropped her hands and started walking toward the door.

I staggered to the truck and my dramatic exit was ruined when I got stuck on the ice a couple of times but I finally managed to navigate back to town.

The apartment's parking lot was a skating rink, as the snow had then turned to freezing rain.

The garbage in the alley was piled high with green bags and cardboard boxes that the fresh produce had been delivered in, bags full of cabbage and rotting meat. I stuck my nose deep into my sweater smelled manure etch- a-sketched on my shirt. No matter how many times I washed the barn off of me, there was always a faint whiff of manure and now Otto or Otter was over in Sweden telling people all Canadian girls smelled like me.

CHAN

Everybody needs a soft spot to fall. Chan's was mine. After I ran away from home, I moved in permanently with Lillian and Elaine and I got hired to work at The China Doll after school and weekends. I loved being a waitress as though it was my calling. I'd take the pencil from behind my ear and write down people's orders, then go in the back and order in a New York accent. Chan said I sounded like my name should be Verna. He also said I was the best waitress he'd ever had. In the past he had a couple of gals, but as soon as he got them trained, they went out and got themselves pregnant, so he'd be back to square one. "Not much good to me, when they have baby in belly. You have no kids. Never put no kids in belly, okay?" With all the brats at home, I felt like I had already raised a family of my own. But still he repeated it to make sure it got through my head, "No babies. You understand me Tamara?"

He called me Tamara because he respected a person's need to start a new life. He was patient with me too as I learned the menu. I don't think it was only because he was a

Christian either. He just seemed to be nice for no good reason.

The first few weeks working there, I taste-tested everything on the menu as long as he made me a side of egg rolls. Chan marveled at how I could eat them with every dish.

"No Chinese eat egg roll," Chan told me. "In fact as child, we eat only things steamed. You Canadians love eating fried things. Very bad for you."

"Why do you cook it for us if you hate it so much?" I asked.

"Because in Rome do as Rome does. In Tel Aviv, do as Tel Aviv does. Hong Kong do as Hong Kong does. You get it?" he asked. Yes I got it. He'd brag to me how hard it was getting Canadians to eat his food at first. "I do everything to keep up business. I fried food and make my own fortune cookies. I could have bought them from distributor, but I am good cook. I tell you what I know. I know Canadians will eat anything, including their fortunes."

It surprised me the number of customers who really believed what the fortune cookies said, as if Chinese people had some connection to the mystical.

Chan used all the mystery to his advantage. His marketing slogan was 'In our restaurant we give you the future to eat.'

The past was always there, haunting him. On the sidewall at the front of the restaurant there was a huge mural hanging above the counter. It was at least 15 feet long and 4 feet high, made of gold plate. It had twenty Chinese people etched on it. Some of the people blew on bugles; some were pulling a cart full of gold coins and jewelry. They looked like happy children on their way to a birthday party, but Chan said they weren't kids at all, just short Chinese men on their way to Canada with big dreams. They looked happy because they were coming to a new land, venturing to start a life of prosperity.

Chan said, "These people in picture going to Montreal

and Toronto to form a place called China Town, a place where they could fit in. But isn't that crazy to go all that way to live exactly like they did in China?"

When I asked him which person he was in the mural he took his Bible and touched the silver milkshake shaker fastened to the wall above the counter.

"I'm way out here, out of the picture. Dolly and I lone wolves," he said, "In Hawley we have nothing. We have no person that we know as home around us. We are big dork."

"You are not big dork, Chan," I said.

"Sure we are but we don't mind. We are big dork that make lots of money. Good business move. No competition here. When you want Chinese food, where you go? You don't say, 'Oh which Chinese place I pick tonight' like they do in Toronto. No you go to the only game in town, The China Doll."

Over the next few weeks, we became very close, gabbing about everything under the sun. I told him about my long list of hates, how I hated school and my mother. How my father had fallen off his pedestal but Chan reassured me that it was normal to hate your parents in Canada.

"See, you all have opportunity to hate your parents. But in China we can't afford to go through normal rebellion, because tradition doesn't allow it. Maybe they are bad parents, maybe they are good, but we were obedient because we give parent respect. In China we know our parents die too soon. But not you in Canada. Your parents live forever because they take vitamins here. Go ahead, despise them. You got luxury of time."

I told him my secret of not capitalizing the name 'jesus'. I was afraid he would be mad at me for that one but he said, "Teenage is time to reject what you grew up with." His parents raised him as a Buddhist, but he said from the time he was a little boy he always wanted to be a Christian, so when he was an adult, he converted.

"Did Dolly convert too?" I asked.

"Yes, Dolly too. Of course she too." Then he shooed me back to work, waving his hand at me like I made a bad smell. A few weeks later when he trusted me a little more he confessed that Dolly was not his sister, but his wife.

"Before we were born, our families decided that we were to be married. The village matchmaker told our parents that it would be good luck for us to be together. Chan said it was his fate to be her husband. He believed in fate, even more than tradition. He said he never looked at another woman, never thought of holding anybody but her his whole life. At sixteen they honored the matchmaker's prophecy and married each other. But on their wedding night when he attempted to touch her, she began to cry.

"She went on like you not believe. I thought her tears would take paint off walls." He laughed and wiped his hands on his apron.

"After many failed attempts, we knew romance not in the cards. Dolly is difficult person, because she is born in the year of the horse. See, in Chinese tradition, the year of the horse is most unlucky for women. Women who are born in year of horse never get man, so her parent lie and say she born in year of pig. But when we are married her true horse come out. So Chan gets a very good idea. I think maybe we can change things, have things go differently if we leave. Not just out of our village, but out of the entire country. I think we should go to Canada. Canadians don't have tradition of matchmakers. They don't have animal signs ruling their destiny so I think good, I can get rid of Dolly. So, we take a ship landing in Toronto, and when officials asked what our relationship to each other was, we said brother and sister. We were processed through immigration that way. I think good. Finally she go her way, and me mine. We will be free. So I picked up my trunk and was dragging it behind me, when I looked back and there she was, standing like her feet were glued to sidewalk. I go back and say 'what wrong' and she say,' I don't know which way to go.' So I take her hand and say 'Come now, you my sister. I don't leave sister alone.'

Toronto was too big for them because there were too many other immigrants. Chan realized he would never stand out in such a big city so one night his father appeared to him in a dream and said. "Go to small place in Canada. Then you be only game in town." Of course he said it in Chinese so Chan could understand him.

So they looked on a map and pointed and their finger landed on Hawley. They came by bus and within weeks had found a building that was perfect for them. It had the restaurant and three small flats, with a shared bathroom down the hall. Dolly could have her own room, and Chan could have his. They were free to come and go as they liked.

If you watched how the two of them operated you'd never know they weren't married. They went mental on each other, just like Nana and JD. Once Dolly was fanning herself saying she was hot and told me to go up to the front and demand he turn the heat down.

When I did he replied,

"It not hot. She born in year of horse. You tell her that." I marched back to the kitchen.

"He says you're not hot, you're horse."

She dropped the dish she was drying and start screaming, "NO!!!! I not horse. He big liar. I a pig. You tell him I A PIG."

Back to the front of the restaurant I went to report, "She says she's not a horse, she's a pig."

Chan started laughing. "Ha. Ha-Ha. Big joke. Jesus know what her true year is." He then waved his Bible in the air as if the Holy Book would settle it once and for all. "Tell her to swear on Bible." So I went back with his Bible and she put her hand on it and whispered the vow he wanted me to extract from her. She looked up to heaven and blessed herself, ripping off a series of Cantonese sentences and then she threw it back at me.

Later when Chan had left for the bank, Dolly curled her finger and motioned for me to move toward her.

"Girl. You, come here. You, come closer," I moved in. She smelled like garbage. "Now listen! You keep secret for Dolly?"

"Sure," I said.

"I swear on Bible. Yes?" She looked at me nodding her head.

I nodded back.

"Well guess what? I don't believe in Bible. He thinks I swear to truth, but I say 'Chan asshole. Chan asshole'. That's what I say but you don't understand because you don't speak my language. Ha. Ha. Ha."

When she laughed you could see her teeth were black in the back. "Bible, it bull shit."

"What?"

"Bull shit. You understand word bull shit?"

"Yes I understand the word, but I thought you were religious."

"No. I go to Church. I pretend because they're nice people. They have nice food. It get me out of house. What else to do? The Bible bull shit. The Buddha bull shit. It all bull shit."

"But why don't you just tell the truth?"

"I tell the truth. Don't you say I am liar! Dolly tell truth, just not to him. He know too much about me, already. Ever since we kids, Chan thinks he knows all my secrets. But there is lots Chan don't know about Dolly – many, many, secrets right? Must keep mystery in my life, right?"

I agreed with her just so she'd get her rotting cabbage smell away from me but before I could deke out of the way, she picked up a cleaver from the drying rack and shook it at me.

"You tell Chan about this and I kill you, okay? I mean it.

I wait until you are asleep and then I come in and chop you up like quail bits."

"What? God. No. I won't tell him." As much as I loved Chan, I wasn't going to die over a job that paid minimum wage.

"I don't want to have to kill you because you are good girl." Then she pulled out a humbug from her pocket and handed it to me. It had pieces of pocket lint stuck to it but I popped it into my mouth and began sucking.

TIPS

When I saw my dad sitting in the booth at the front, I thought he'd come to town to beg me to come home. "Hello sir, may I help you." I pulled out my pad.

"Don't be a damn donkey."

"What sir?" I asked, trying to keep this professional.

"You're better than this."

"Better than what?"

"Working at this kind of place for people's hand outs."

"You mean tips?"

"Only hookers get tips."

"Honest to God. Where did you hear that?"

"If you can't afford to be on your own you should just come home and forget about it. You and your Mother should get along."

"Look if Alberta sent you, you can tell her..."

"No. She doesn't know where I am."

"Really?"

"No. I came into town with JD."

"She didn't send you?" My shoulders slumped.

"No! You know how your mother gets. She's not going to beg."

"Why not," she begged Lillian.

"The boys are getting the hang of things. Patrick is as strong as an ox."

"Well, it's nice her slaves are so easily replaced," I shot back.

"Your mother is taking a university course. Did you know that?"

"No."

"She started back a few months ago, so she can go back to teaching soon. She's got this one book that's all about reverse psychology."

"OK."

"She tells people one thing and she means another. When she says I burn her ass she might mean the opposite. She might want to kiss it." He laughs at his own joke.

"So her not coming means she really is worried about me."

"Look, there's your version of things Tammy and there's my version of things and somewhere in the middle is the truth. You know what I'm saying?"

I hadn't been able to follow one damn thing he was saying since he sat down.

"What can I get you, Dad?"

"I have no idea. I don't know what half this stuff is."

As he flipped through the big plastic sheets of the menu, Elaine came in from the bank and sat down beside him. "Hey how are you doing, King?"

"Right now, I am confused about what to eat."

"The Dop Gai Pai Woey is good." I suggested. "And maybe an egg roll."

King yelled a question at Chan who just stood there reading his Bible. "Have these egg rolls got cat in them?"

"We out of cat today," Chan said without missing a

beat.

"Pretty funny for a Chinaman." King leaned in, "So there's no cat?"

"There is no cat," I couldn't believe he was so ignorant. "They're egg rolls. We get them from the supplier in Toronto."

"Well no, I don't think I'll risk it. I'll have fish and chips with ketchup," said King. "And can I get a pot of tea? Do you have normal Canadian tea?"

"Yes, we got tea." Chan replied.

"Good, I would like fish and chips. And tea with milk and sugar." Chan bowed to him and hustled into the back to make the order.

While we waited, we had to listen to King tell us about the big project he was getting into in the spring. Something to do with a car wash he'd like to invest in and how he wanted to get in on the ground floor. It was a real money maker that we could help him run; one more idea that was going to make him a millionaire.

He turned to me and said, "Cause, you never know eh Tam? Your old dad might make it big one day, before it's all over." King was talking this way and that. I didn't have time to figure it all out because Chan dinged the bell in back. Heading to pick up his order, I saw Lillian come down the stairs for her afternoon shift at the nursing home.

"What a surprise to see you, King. How are you?"

"I feel like a million bucks," King said. "And I've got some news. Boots got back from the spin dry up north."

"Spin dry?"

"Treatment. When I drove him up there they said they'd never seen a man in that kind of shape ever recover and well, now he's back."

"That was a long way for you to take him in the first place." Her face was pinched.

"Well it's a fair hike. Dragged me out a bit, but I got to see a beautiful part of the world. The northerners are pretty friendly people. I'd like buy a piece of land up there some day just to have it, you know as an investment for the kids when they grow up? Well this time he lasted the whole stint."

"No. Well isn't that something. That's wonderful." She was saying wonderful but shaking her head no.

"Thirty days is something eh Maw? " Elaine turned to my Dad, "Right King?"

"That's right. He's dry as a twig. You don't want to light a match near him" he joked.

"You knew he went?" Lillian's head snapped toward Elaine.

"I heard through the grapevine." Elaine jumped in.

"Must have done some good," my father stammered. "They tightened a few screws he had loose. Now they say he's going to have a long road ahead of him. According to them he's not right in the head. They say he'll be foggy for awhile. They say once they put down the booze, it takes time to thaw out, you know?"

Lillian didn't say anything.

"It's all good, right Lillian? King asked. "It's what you wanted."

"That's not all I wanted" Lillian said." I wanted a lot more than that King."

"Well I mean you didn't want him to be an alcoholic no more. But that's the problem with that side of the family. They're alcoholics. My side are just drunks." King cracked up at his own joke but nobody laughed with him. There was an awkward silence, then Lillian said:

"Thanks King, you're good to have come into town to tell us this. But I have to get to work. I'm going to be late." She kept smiling and she turned around and instead of going out the front door she went to the kitchen. I could hear Dolly screeching at her through the porthole.

When I handed Dad the bill, he looked back at the kitchen to make sure Lillian was out of earshot.

"Well I can see that didn't sit too well. Guess putting a word in for the man is all I can do."

"You came because of him?" I asked but he seemed not to hear me as he was looking into the hole in the door to the back kitchen. He yelled at Chan "HOW MUCH DO I OWE YOU?"

"FIVE-FIFTY." Chan yelled back but King didn't get that he was being mocked .

King turned to me and said something I will never forget.

"You know in a few years I am going to look a lot smarter than I do right now."

He was wrong about that, completely and utterly wrong.

FIRED

There is no job worse than cleaning the lids of the sweet and sour containers. I was running the tap water through the tiny hole of a lid while Lillian sat on a bar stool, a suitcase beside her.

"I don't think I can do it again Chan, not again."

Chan had a look in his eyes like he was going to kiss her. If he intended to, he never got the chance because at that moment, Dolly charged in with her a suitcase of her own. She tugged on Lillian's sleeve. "Let's go, let's go," then ripped the suitcase out from under Lillian and dragged it toward the door. "What you got in here. Dead body? Bus is coming and it won't wait."

As they disappeared down the street, you could hear Lillian saying, over and over again. "Oh Dolly, Dolly, Dolly."

Yes, crazy gets you to say its name in every sentence. The Greyhound bus pulled in down the street and they got on, another set of women running away from home. I watched Chan wipe his eyes but there were no tears. Sometimes despair and relief exist in the same exhale.

I ran up to the apartment to inform Elaine of the latest development. She was sitting at the kitchen table like the queen in the counting house, counting all her money. She glanced up.

"Well, I see you know about the latest departures," she said.

Ben, still in his postal uniform, staggered out of the smoke-filled bathroom. He'd hot-boxed it by closing all the windows and doors and putting towels on the bottom of the door. He was baked.

"They broke away on the freedom train," he mumbled.

Elaine picked up the money and put the queen's faces all in the same direction. "Chan will miss his lover girl."

"Dolly and he are not together," I said.

"I meant Lillian. He had the hots for my mother."

"Get out!" Ben laughed. "My man Chan wouldn't hustle your mother."

"Oh he's a man just like the rest of you," Elaine snorted.

"No offence, Ben."

"None taken," he laughed at a spot on his shirt and continued. "If you ask me, I think Lillian and Dolly were the ones who had something going."

"Shut your mouth," said Elaine. "I don't need that image in my head.

"Why? Are you prejudiced against lesbians?" he asked.

"Look, they're not lesbians because they're not that interesting."

"Tammy, tell her to stop messing up my head."

"I don't know what either one of you is talking about." I poured myself some Tia Maria and mixed it with a coffee, "Where are Dolly and Lillian going anyway? That's what I want to know."

"Scarborough. There's a safe house that's like the underground railroad for women. I don't know what she wants. He isn't crazy when he's not drinking. He hasn't come near her at all."

"Well he doesn't need to." Ben argued. "Angry men repress their victims just by their presence. Once they've done the violence they can control by just a look."

He looked quite impressed with himself for a moment, then a blank look came over his face like someone had taken an eraser and wiped his mind clean. "What was I saying?"

"You were saying, what was she supposed to do? Stick around and hope for the best?" I interpreted that for him because it's what I felt too.

"I did? Wow. Cool." He laughed.

Elaine started pacing. "He just got back and he's already being rejected," she said.

"Elaine, how can you say that?" I couldn't follow her reasoning.

"They need to split or it'll be the same old story again," Ben repeated.

"I'm talking about her. He has nothing to do with it."

"He has everything to do with it."

"He's nowhere near her. She's in town. He's out there. We were perfectly fine."

"But he could come for her anytime, and how would she protect herself?"

"The way she always has. Me." Elaine waved a handful of twenties at him

"He tried to kill you both, Elaine."

She turned to me, "You tell him this?"

"No."

"What? You think you're invisible?" Ben continued because he was stoned and didn't value his life. "I know he shot the dog."

"How the fuck -?"

"It's a small town, Elaine. Everyone knows he's violent."

"He shot one dog, one time. It was a mistake. He never got that bad again.'

I piped in, "Elaine you sat in our driveway night after night."

Ben continued: "He didn't need to. Shooting a dog keeps people in line."

"Shut up, Ben."

"All I'm saying is I support her decision to take off."

"Well good for you," she said, "Show your support some other place."

"Elaine, man you are not listening," he repeated, "I said support. I'm supporting her decision," but Elaine walked over and put her hand over his mouth.

"SHUTUP. Look you faggot you say one more word you gay lord, and I'll kill you."

"It is a very positive reinforcing word. Tell her Tammy, did I not say the word support?"

"SHUT UP. "Elaine yelled.

"Ben, maybe we should drop it." I said.

"GET OUT. You fricking fagolahomesexualsapien" she said in some foreign gibberish as he covered his head to protect himself from her abuse.

"Chill man, chill" he repeated over and over again but this howl came out of her. "ZAAAAAAAAAAA." Dogs from other counties could hear her.

"Go, Ben. Just go." I handed him a baggie of weed as motivation.

"I said support," he repeated, standing up, "I'm on your side. I support..."

"ZAAAAAAAAAAAAAAAAAAAAA," she screamed.

Chan banged on the ceiling below. Ben staggered toward the door and then tried to slam it but he was stoned so it shut softly and we could him mumbling as he disappeared. Elaine returned to the table to count her cash again. Counting twenties calmed her. I took the scoop from the flour tin, washed and dried it, then took the pot and weighed it and put it in Baggies with twist ties around the top. We sat there for ten minutes before she spoke again.

"He's missing the whole point. The problem is she doesn't know what she wants. I mean, I get used to the car and she sends me to your house. I get used to that, I get sent home. Then I get to go out west with Raju and Jinsa. They get me tested."

"For drugs?"

"For brains. Turns out, I got a high IQ.. So they put me in this brainer school and I get used to that. But no, she wants me back. So I come home. Now she's a Christian and we come here. I'm getting used to…". She stopped mid-sentence, her eyes twitching. "She better not think I'm going up to Toronto on some rescue mission."

"Elaine, I'm sorry." I said and I really was. I put my hand on top of hers but she licked it, "Don't you feel sorry for me."

"I'm not."

"Don't give me that pity-face. I hate it."

"Okay."

"You're just as nuts as me."

"No I am not."

"It was a compliment." She sat down on the couch and changed the subject. "You know what I don't understand? Why do people give the poor their ugly shit? Look at this couch".

"I'm not nuts."

"Poor people aren't supposed to have any taste." She ripped up her deposit slip, stuffed the pile of cash in her pocket and put on her coat. "Well screw that. Come on. You and I are getting rid of that ugly-assed couch."

She pulled on her jacket and we went down to Sears where she ordered a new couch from the fall catalogue. Elaine got rid of a couch, her mother and Ben in the same day. Ben tried to get back in, said he was too stoned to know what he was talking about, but Elaine will not let anyone say they're sorry. I can attest to that.

She put him out of the game he started, took over the drug selling and all his clients just like that. There isn't much customer loyalty in that business.

The new couch was delivered and I didn't dare sit on it in case I spilled something. It was just like being back home.

BUFFET

Chan tried to keep up the same pace but the work was overwhelming. Dolly had done so many things I hadn't noticed. Besides the obvious things like the dishes, she had taken inventory, ordered and kept the kitchen clean. These responsibilities fell to me. I tried to convince Chan to close for a day so we could catch up – Mondays and Tuesdays were dead – but he refused. We stayed open no matter what. Sometimes on Mondays he would go upstairs to his apartment to have a nap. That meant I was there alone. There was no shortage of things to do, but it was boring, mind-numbing work.

One Monday we got a new shipment of placemats.

Each placement had an alphabetical list of cocktails with instructions on how to make each one: Absinthe, Black Russian, Bloody Mary, Rob Roy, Singapore Sling. When I saw those placemats, the devil got in me. I decided I should try all the drinks myself. The Absinthe went down easy. So did the Bloody Mary, and the Bacardi was so good, I had two. By the time I got to the Drambuie I was shitfaced.

Chan came down a couple of hours later and found me passed out. He must have dragged me up to the apartment for when I came to I was under the covers, fully clothed. The next day, I apologized. Chan laughed it off.

'My fault. I buy placemats and they give you bad ideas. Luckily you only got to 'G' - Gin. Yuck. But I don't blame you. I take it out of your pay cheque. Ha Ha. Chan joke.'

It makes it worse when people understand you. If he had yelled I could have gotten mad but his being nice drove me nuts. I felt like I owed him something, so I started pretending being a waitress was the most important thing in my life.

As it is with most things, you find yourself believing what you thought you were faking. One Monday, five words came into my mind that I actually got excited about. Those words were 'All-you-can-eat Buffet.' Nobody in town had one and certainly there had never been a Chinese All-you-can-eat Buffet.'

"Can we Chan? Huh Chan? Huh?"

He shot the idea down right away but I kept repeating the idea until it got through his thick head. What sold him was when I told him how much money he could save by cooking in bulk one night a week. Chan wanted it to be held on Fridays, but that wasn't smart as the fish and chip place already had that business locked with the Catholics. We agreed Saturday night was best and I made a sign with happy faces and Chinese characters in the border. I taped it up in the front window and dropped off photocopies of the menu at different stores and stuck them on people's windshields when they were shopping.

Elaine gave me one piece of good advice - set the price low to draw the people in. We priced it right, at $4.95, which even in those days was fair and square. Anybody could afford that price and once I got them in the door I could sell customers drinks and tea and take out. We agreed on a simple menu: Sweet and Sour Spare Ribs, Sweet and Sour Chicken, and Beef and Oyster Sauce. Chan put the rice at the front of the line of the buffet with the egg rolls so people would fill up their plates with the cheaper stuff. We took turns spooning out the meat dishes so we could control portions. I had one rule only for the buffet, and that was no green Jell-O. The over-use of Jell-O is the sign of a very poor buffet.

The first week Elaine counted 28 customers. People came in when the door opened at 4:00 PM. They were all old folks who wanted to eat and get out before 5:30 PM Saturday night mass. They also had to make sure their last bite was taken an hour before communion was served. Old people are very aggressive. They'd butt in the line-up and get annoyed if I didn't dish up enough meat. I swear some of them starved themselves all week to get their money's worth.

After the first rush, there was be a smattering of couples and families until another good rush came in around 6:30 PM when mass got out. I didn't stop for eight hours, running back and forth from kitchen to the buffet station, refilling tubs of buffet items. I had to keep loading the dishwasher to keep up. It was a madhouse from the time we opened at noon until we closed at 2:00 am. I told Chan that if this kept up, we could start closing early Saturday nights and not have to stay open late for the bar gang. The drunks never tipped. But no, Chan said he would cook more buffet items and let the drunks eat the leftovers. They were too loaded to care if the food had been sitting in the steam table for hours and he would make a higher profit.

I started the buffet to look good but soon it became a personal mission to educate the palates of Hawley. These yahoos needed to be more open-minded when it came to eating. I believed it then. I believe it now. The more you eat from another person's culture the less chance there is you'll kill them. Think of all the wars that would be avoided if people would try the food of that culture. Each week, I put out the regular fare as well as small portions of traditional Chinese dishes. I stuck it on the same serving tray as the items they knew so they would put it on their plate without knowing what they were getting. One week it was Egg Foo Yong. One time I even tried quail bits. Chan worried about that too. What if town people heard he was serving quail? They'd gossip about him.

"They already gossip about you, Chan," I said. "They say you serve cat. Quail would be a step up."

"Clever girl," he chuckled.

He called me his sous-chef. I cut and chopped all the vegetables and meats for the dishes and got the food ready for him to do his magic. I tried to eyeball the amount of spices he threw in, but like all good cooks, he was secretive about precise measurements. Yet I watched and recorded all of the spices he used when he wasn't looking.

We had only one argument and it wasn't over me drinking his booze. No it was over, of all things, rice pudding. Even though the Chinese are a very talented nation, dessert is not one of their strong points.

One day I said: "Rice pudding would be a nice addition to the menu." His head nearly swung off its axis. He said rice was not a thing anyone would eat for desert. No matter how many recipes I showed him as evidence to the contrary, he couldn't get his head around it. He got so upset he barely spoke to me for two days. I went behind his back and made a batch anyway. I cooked it up in the apartment and filled about ten little sundae dishes with it. I even put a red cherry on top. By the time he saw it on the buffet station, we had almost run out of the stuff. He still argued but the victory came when I got him to try it. He scrunched up his face and held his breath and the next week I caught him eating an extra dish when he thought I wasn't looking.

Chan seemed to be getting out of his funk over Dolly and Lillian. He'd stopped singing Catholic hymns in Chinese.

I was making good money for my age, which should have

made me happy too. I was okay when it was busy but when it slowed down a black cloud hit me in the face. Mid-afternoons were the worst. When school got out, puck bunny girls with names like Clara and Bonnie came in to gab. Best friends, pushing French Fries around their plates, discussing a teacher they hated or the school dance that was coming up. When I listened to them

I had to stand with both hands on the inside of the doorway pushing back the walls from crushing me.

My life was taking a different path. I had been to The Cadillac, and had sex on an international level and the following week I would meet a stripper with two vaginas. Who could possibly go back to school?

SNOW

The Cadillac got strippers because people got sick of Suitcase Ray playing the same tunes over and over again. He claimed he had fifty songs in his repertoire, but forty-eight of them were by Johnny Cash. Frank, the owner, told him if he couldn't learn some new songs he'd have to let him go but Ray wouldn't let anyone mess with his artistic integrity. After Frank fired Ray, he had to find a different entertainment option for Thursday Nights.

Thanks to his friend, Blacky, he came up with the idea of strippers.

From the first minute people heard about the naked women, the bar was packed with men from three counties over. The roads could be impassable, snow blowing fiercely, but by God they dug themselves out and drove to town. They weren't going to miss that action.

If I ever end up going to university, I will write a paper on the kind of men who look at strippers. They fall into three categories. One type comes to criticize. These guys are the kind that sit there and complain, "She doesn't look like her picture. She's a bit chunky, isn't she?"

It was true, some of the girls were a bit bruised or didn't keep up their dye jobs, but what did these men expect? They should have been grateful. Fat blobs themselves, big-bellied bruisers who looked like they were about to give birth. Not one of them had ever seen a woman naked like that except on a calendar at the mechanic's shop.

The second type acted like he didn't know what he was getting into. He'd come in for a drink, was sitting there innocently having a beer when a woman started taking her clothes off in front of him. That's what he would have told the priest or his wife he had got caught.

"I was just having a pint of draft, Father."

"Honest to God, honey cheeks, I was just sitting there minding my own beeswax and before I knew it, there was a naked woman doing a kitchy koo dance in front of me."

The third kind liked to pretend they weren't watching at all. They'd talk all the way through the girl's routines. Once in a while they'd look up, but for the most part a woman's crotch could be planted smack dab in the middle of their face, and still all they would do is talk about how hard it was to get the corn planted with all the rain, and how their tractor broke down again and they had to go to town to get a part but the John Deer place didn't have it in so it had to be placed on order.

It was fascinating to me, how those women could be so confident, so at ease with nothing but their birthday suits on. I couldn't take my eyes off of them. I didn't want to touch their breasts. I wanted to have their breasts.

For a few weeks, different groups of strippers came to shake things up, but then one group came and stayed: The Cunning Stunts. Three dancers were featured under that title. There were two warm up girls and the lead dancer, Snow. Snow was a beautiful caramel-skinned girl, eyelashes thick with black mascara. She looked like she had been born to stand up there with a piece of material covering her triangle. Blacky gave me the scoop; she had worked her way up, dancing in the strip joints in Quebec, but her real claim to fame was her two vaginas.

"I don't know how they work," he scratched his head in confusion, "Maybe she has one vagina and another in the trunk in case she gets a flat. Or is it more like a generator on the farm? If there is a storm and the electricity goes out the second one takes over."

I too wondered about the problem two vaginas would pose for the singled minded penis.

One Thursday I got introduced to Snow. I was nursing my brew, and she was doing the cobra arch on the carpet when our eyes met. She shimmied down on her belly to the front of the stage.

"I'm Snow."

"Tammy."

She reached her hand for mine. I didn't touch it because I wasn't sure it was clean.

The drum machine pounded out a mind numbing rhythm, and the men talked on in the background. Nobody seemed to notice us carrying on a conversation.

"Real nice bunch of men we got here tonight," she ventured.

"Yes! I apologize for my people." I said and she laughed.

"I am so bored." She looked at one of the men and stuck her tongue out in a sexy way and flicked it in his direction.

"I mean, this isn't Montreal."

"There is always something exciting going on. I love Montreal men. Don't you?"

"I kind of prefer the Swedish."

"Really? Aren't you exotic? Never had myself any Swedish man!" She laughed and marched to the other side of the stage. She arched her back and thrust her crotch at Blacky who put a dollar bill in her g-string.

"I'm sure Montreal men are nice, too." I called out and she moved back toward me.

"Hell, no. But that's what I love about them. They don't pretend to be. Not like these guys who act like they're family men. These losers will get up tomorrow and pretend they were never in here. In Montreal, the men are not pussies. They admit they like strippers. Ever heard of Pointe Claire? Well I'm going with one of the guys from there and he rides a hog. You know?" She leaned into me and whispered, "Riding with him has really helped my spread." She sat on the floor and demonstrated how far her legs could open - a perfect V. "I'm a trained ballerina," she yelled at the men at the bar but they continued drinking. "You ever heard of the National Ballet?"

"Sure," I said.

"You're looking at their lead dancer." She yelled.

"Wow. That's neat." I yelled back.

"Ever hear of Swan Lake?"

"You danced in Swan Lake?"

"Ever heard of Karen Kain? "

"Yeah" I lied.

"Well, guess who was her understudy? That's right, you're looking at her."

"So you danced for Karen Kain?"

"That broad never took a night off. She'd haul her sorry ass out of bed no matter how sick she was. Infect everybody around her with some flu bug and go on truckin'. Can't blame her. She was a star and only had so many good years before her legs were going to seize up but I got sick of waiting for her to break an ankle, so I started choreographing my own dances and one thing led to another."

"It must be a step down playing in a dump like this." I said.

"There are no small places, just small strippers. I say that to the girls every night before we go on. Because every gig builds your resume, you know? Besides I'm in charge of my own life. Karen Kain can go screw herself. "

"So you don't mind the naked part?"

"No. That doesn't bug me. What gets to me, is they are taking the art out of it. They want us to sit on some guy's crotch and dry hump him."

"That's perverted." I said looking around imagining and quickly picked out the ones who would sign up for that.

You know it's time to get out of the business when that crotch shit starts." She pointed to a ring on her left hand. "It's my engagement ring from my Angel. Snow went on to explain that he was 'trying out' for the Hell's Angel, going through an initiation period where they audition new prospects. Hell's Angels have sponsors just like they do in the double A's. The difference is, you called your sponsor in AA if you're tempted to be bad. In The Hell's Angels you call if you're tempted to be good.

"When he gets accepted, we're getting married. He wanted me to shack up but screw that."

"Yeah screw that." I agreed.

"We've got a big wedding planned for next year. My mother is going crazy inviting people. She's invited half of Parry Sound. I'm going to have six bridesmaids so I don't need to be running around in a ballet company doing the dance of the dying swan. Who needs the tragedy? The swan dies did you know that?"

"Oh wow. Does she?" I couldn't believe how much she knew.

"She gets shot by a hunter."

"Probably one of these guys in here." I looked at Blacky who at that moment was doing armpit farts. "They always hunt out of season."

"You are so hilarious. Hey you want to come backstage some time?"

"Sure." Becoming friends with a stripper wasn't something I had on my list of things to do but when one asks you to come back stage, you can't refuse. It would make a good memory when sucking on Saltines in the nursing home.

"Come around next Thursday." Then she stood up ripped off her bra, naked except for the g-string. The music died down as she pranced off the stage.

I was the only one clapping.

When I told Elaine of the superstar I'd met, she claimed she and Snow had already run into each other at the bank when they were making deposits. I didn't want to bring her along, but after Lillian and Ben had vamoosed, she was cranky twenty-four seven.

We got into a regular set-to over what gift to bring for Snow. We couldn't go empty handed to an entertainer's back door.

I wanted to bring something homemade because being on the road so much I thought she'd appreciate baking. Elaine thought she'd appreciate the drugs, so we baked hash brownies. I added mayonnaise because hash dries out the brownie terribly. After last call, there we stood, two star-struck fans. It's embarrassing to think how simple we must have looked, standing there dressed to the nines, holding our offering in its plastic case. Even when filled with hash brownies, Tupperware dials down the cool factor.

A monster of a guy with a handle bar moustache shepherded us into a dingy, back room. It smelled of crotch. There were groupies back there, a bunch of men fawning over the Stunts. Snow sat with a kimono draped over her, but it wasn't covering much. It made me cold just looking at her. It was freezing back there but she wasn't shivering.

"Sorry for the paltry condition of my dressing room," she apologized. "A lot of the small towns want us to come to dance, but they don't have a big enough set-up to accommodate us. The other Stunts are bitching to me about it; say they'll catch their death of cold. I tell them 'girls it will keep your skin looking tighter'." She yelled her over shoulder.

"It's a free face lift, isn't that right Gordy?"

Gordy, the dullard who had escorted us in, let go an ignorant burp. Snow turned back to us and said. "He says I should start a union, but jeez when would I ever get the time for that?"

"Who are you?" Elaine asked. Gordy's veins bulged in his neck.

Snow giggled and started rubbing his stomach,

"There, there, baby. Why, he's my angel, girls."

"Gordy Keith," he put out his hand. "I'm her agent and fiancé. Who the frig are you?"

"Elaine Cochrane. I run this town," Elaine said flipping her hair back over her shoulder and held out her hand to shake his. He held it far too long.

We handed Snow our present but she tossed it on the make-up table and gave us hell for bringing it. Gordy explained she couldn't eat chocolate or hash because she'd gain twenty pounds just looking at it.

"Don't take offense," Snow explained, "It's just that my body is my temple and I have to put only sacred life-affirming things in it.

She stood up and turned up her stereo system. Marvin Gaye was singing 'Let's Get It On'. The party was happening when Elaine blurted out: "Do you really have a double vagina?"

Snow stared at her from the makeup mirror. Gordy's face darkened but Elaine didn't flinch.

"That story got started after I spent a night with this band called the Pea Coats. They're a bunch of losers doing Beatle cover music. I had a one-night-stand with the drummer but it didn't go so well." She took her finger and made it droop. "So he started a rumor about my wahooy."

"So she doesn't have a double vagina?"

"Of course she does," Gordy said, "but she doesn't need some two bit musician blabbing about it."

"Its okay sweetie, Mama's learned her lesson." She rubbed Gordy's forearm.

"Never date a drummer."

"That's right babe," he said, turning back to Elaine. "Musicians will give you a bad reputation."

"Well," said Elaine, "Having a bad one is better than no reputation at all."

Gordy smiled, "Hey I like your style." Elaine dropped her head.

"I ain't got no style. I just got me."

Gordy nodded to Snow who reached into the pocket of her kimono and pulled out a blue sachet that she unfolded onto the make up table. Inside there was a mirror, razor blade and a bag of white powder. Snow cut the cocaine into four lines, pulled out a dollar bill from her G-string and rolled it into a funnel. She bent over and breathed a line into her right nostril, then the left. Gordy took his turn and redid the mirror. As he passed the mirror to me everything began moving in slow motion. I knew one nostril full would be the end of me. When I shot up a couple of Hail Mary's the BVM must have been on duty because somehow I shook my head no. Gordy tensed his thick neck and looked at Elaine.

"She don't party?"

I looked at Elaine as well, pleading for help with my eyes. She smiled at Gordy.

"You don't want her doing any of that shit. Look at her. She's paranoid enough."

He shook his head in disgust, and offered my line to Elaine. She had a decision to make. Two of us couldn't refuse so she placed a finger in the white powder and rubbed it on her gums.

"Is it pure?" she asked.

Gordy nodded.

"You sure it's not laced with anything?"

Gordy laughed, "Pure as the driven Snow."

I was sitting on the couch behind Elaine. She had on a backless macramé halter-top so when she bent over I could see every muscle in her back tighten. Slowly, she inhaled a line. I breathed with her as she took one nostril full, then the second. I got high just watching her. When she sat up, I got a head rush. My heart was racing because one person doesn't do coke, the whole room does. The energy ramps up like everything is about to go off the rails.

Whatever it looked like from the outside, this was far more than a casual interchange with a two-bit dancer and her boyfriend. Opportunity was banging on the door. Elaine had realized quickly you don't get far selling dime bags to high school kids. That night she could smell where the real money was.

Elaine had to find out the chain of command. Even I could see that Snow wasn't the dealer. She kept on going that night long after Gordy had stopped. A dealer couldn't put that much up her nose and stay in business. Snow was working for someone else and it didn't take a genius to see it was bulldog Gordy, so Elaine waited and watched. He came some weeks with Snow and some weeks he kept his distance. When he was there, Elaine fawned over the couple asking about their upcoming wedding. She gushed over the diamond ring which Gordy had designed for Snow when he took a jewelry-making course.

"Well aren't you creative?" Elaine fawned.

"After all I thought I could design a diamond ring. I did toos." He smacked his lips.

"Toos?" Elaine was confused.

"Tattoos." He took off his shirt. He was built, each muscle clearly defined. I might have been interested if it wasn't covered in snakes with different women's names on them. He started to rhyme them off.

"And that was Coco, she was a gal from Point Claire." He winked. "She had joie de vivre."

Elaine said. “I’d like to get me some of that.”

“Ah, Coco was a douche bag,” Snow said.

He ignored her comment and went on about the damn ring and how if he designed it, it would be half the cost of a jewelry store rock.

Each week I sat there on the couch, with my sunglasses on. If they couldn’t see the whites of my eyes I could keep below the radar. I knew I had truly disappeared when one of the Stunts plunked down and it took her at least ten seconds to notice she was sitting on me. It was like being a bartender listening in on people’s conversation

Selling coke is a pyramid scheme. There are the big guys at the top and peons at the bottom. The big guys want to be as far away from the small time dealers as possible so nothing can get traced back to them. Instead of a Pink Cadillac, you get a jail sentence.

Snow confessed that she’d been bringing in small amounts of cocaine over the last few months, and if she did get caught she had a strategy. Apparently there was some use for that second vagina after all. She’d been checking out Hawley to see whether there were enough customers. Seems there were. All she needed now was a good distributor.

The next time Gordy appeared in town, Elaine knew she was being tested, being groomed as that distributor, so she refused to do any lines.

“Some spend money. Others make it.” Elaine kept her eyes on Gordy. “You might ask yourself which side of the line you want me on?”

Snow stared at her like she had three heads.

“I think you’re taking the concept too far, Elaine,” then she inhaled Elaine’s share.

Elaine winked at him and he must have liked what he heard because the next week when we went back stage Snow tossed a bag of the white stuff at her.

“See what you can do.” Snow said. Elaine had a week to

prove herself.

Locating coke customers is like finding ants at a picnic. You show up with a hamper and they arrive out of nowhere. With pot you can sell anywhere, but coke is secretive. You don't want customers showing up on the fire escape or knocking on your door at four in the morning. People need to make an appointment.

Elaine's clients were an odd mixture. There were migrant workers who stayed at the motel on the old Trans Canada, the ones that were in construction and had ready cash came often. But there were also some folks I knew from 4-H: girls who looked like they were going to baste a hem. Good people with good parents: Marcus Topping who had the ride-on lawn mower; even one of the Everett Boys. He was full of shame when he saw me. "Don't tell my brother," he said. Even though he saw me flashing my boobs for the pizza guy, he still thought of me as Tammy Babcock from Catechism class.

I was innocent. I didn't think I was an accomplice. In fact, had I been arrested and given a lie detector test, I would have passed easily. I believed I was just some farm girl with fat knees watching while Elaine played host to a bunch of high-strung men with mirrors in their pockets.

LAID

I was having a really good sex dream when the phone rang. It was my brother Patrick. “Get to the hospital, right now,” he said. “It’s Dad.”

Half asleep, I thought he meant my grandfather, J.D. but when I got to Furlong Hospital, I found out it was King. When I walked into the room there he was hooked up to the oxygen tank, skin was yellow. He’d woken in the middle of the night, gasping for breath. He thought it was his nerves so he made some of Nana’s warm milk concoction but that didn’t help.

Alberta said he’d been coughing up blood all night but even then the knot-head wouldn’t go to the doctor. He practically had to be doubled over before he’d let my mother take him to the hospital. At the E.R. they took one look at him and put him in a wheelchair. They did blood work and tests and by morning he was in the operating room. His oesophagus had haemorrhaged. Doctors came in packs with clipboards and began shaking their heads and saying: ‘We warned him. We said it would spread.” Stupidly I thought all that smoking had finally caught up with him. Then they said the C Word.

Stage One. Two. Three. I hated math – never understood numbers – and the doctors didn't help make it easier. There was so much information coming at us, so much to understand. One minute he was well and there was lots of time to be mad at him and the next he was sick and there was nothing they could do.

Stage four. Not a good number.

J.D. and Nana sat in the corner. King's parents didn't come because they didn't do that sort of thing. Entering a hospital spooked them – thought they might get in and never get out.

"Hey, Suzie." I looked up. I thought J.D. was talking to me but it was Alberta he was addressing. "What are you doing about that bloated cow?"

"Going to have to lance it," she answered. They went on about how they were going to have to put a tube up its ass so it could let go a fart. Not an appropriate conversation at the best of times, but certainly not at someone's sick bed. And especially the sickbed of my dad who hated cows to begin with. But that's family for you. They're no more considerate when you're dying than they are when you're living.

I remember Marley and the boys wailing but I didn't cry. There were tears but they were lodged in granite. Then Patrick yelled: "You're not dying. Dad, you're not dying, I won't let you," as if bad news would listen to protests. Trying to hold off death is as pointless as trying to hold off birth, as pointless as sitting on the passenger side trying to slow down the driver by braking with your foot.

My mind filled with an endless loop of imagining. When I left home, did they know then? Was it a secret they kept between the two of them? Why had no one warned me before I told him off?

Guilt washed over me. I wished I could take back the accusations of him being a lazy father. He was likely lying on the couch because he didn't feel well. Why couldn't I have just shut my mouth? I wondered if that was what he was trying to tell me when he came to the restaurant. When he said, "There's your version of things and my version of things and then there's the truth," maybe that was his big hint he should have made it clearer. He should have said, "Truth is, I'm sick and want you to come back before I croak." But King spoke in a cryptic language his whole life. He expected me to read between the lines like I was a mind reader.

When they stabilized him, they sent him back to the house and because he couldn't do the stairs they put the bed in the good living room. People took turns tending to his needs with the help of a VON student nurse who came every day. Elaine and I never left him.

He would sit on the bed hunched over, barely able to get his breath despite the oxygen he was huffing.

Half the county showed up with casseroles. We practically had to book an appointment to see him. Men from two counties around came to shoot the breeze. They knew it was too late to implement any of his big ideas but they liked listening to him and holding court made him feel like he was still the same man. No matter how bad a time he was having, when they came in the room he would sit up and act like nothing was wrong. He put on quite the performance until the last couple of days. We had to meet them at the door and say he wasn't up for a visit.

Many nights Elaine and I stayed beside him and slept on the floor. In case he had a turn for the worse, we wanted to be on hand. Both of us were trying to get every last drop of the man we knew as father. There were never going to be enough good-byes. Elaine got who King was. She knew what made him tick better than I ever did. I made him nervous because I was always trying to please him and make him proud but she sat with him and expected nothing. She had a directness King liked.

She shaved him, showed him his clean face in the hand mirror.

"Thanks, 'Lainy." He squeezed her hand.

"You're welcome, Uncle King. Look at that handsome face."

"I look like death warmed over."

"Well, you don't look any hell do you?"

"No shit, Shakespeare," he said.

"King, are you scared of dying?"

"I get scared of not breathing. Sometimes in the middle of the night, you know, I get a panic in me..." His words trailed off. Elaine poured some sour looking liquid from a brown bottle into his coffee cup and held it to his lips. Alberta welled up, saying: "Enough of this depressing conversation." For Alberta, talking about dying was giving it permission to come in and take a seat.

"I would be scared, too," Elaine continued.

"I said he doesn't need to be stirred up, Elaine," Alberta reiterated.

"No, he doesn't." I agreed Alberta for the first time in months.

King took my mother's hand and said, "Look Alberta, I'm not dead yet. In fact I was thinking of running suckers in a couple of weeks. We could go on a date out there. Take a picnic. Take the kids. What do you say, lover?"

"Some date. Five kids with us?"

"Oh well they won't bother us, lover."

"I don't know, King."

"Why not?"

"It's too early in the spring." The way she said it soft like that scared me. "It makes me cold just thinking about it."

"That was how I got your mother to marry me, girls. She was charmed by my ability to run suckers."

"Yes, weren't you a big Casanova?" Alberta let a smile ooze out.

"We should go right now, Alberta." He sat up and held his side.

"You can't, King." Alberta laid him gently down.

"I will go with you, King." Elaine said.

"Tammy, you want to come?" he asked.

I don't know why, but I said, "I hate fishing." I did hate it, but why could I not have said yes? I couldn't stop myself from being difficult.

"You used to love it before you got so independent. At the first sign of spring we'd take the nets out and run them upstream. When you two were barely three, we went to the workman's co-op and bought the both of you little kid boots and we couldn't get you out of that river."

"I shudder to think about it." Alberta shook her head.

"We convinced your mothers to let us take you to the river – further down from where we swim where it runs quicker, you know, where the falls are?"

"I almost got sick to my stomach," Alberta laughed.

"Your mother and Lillian were convinced you'd drown, but we took care of you. We kept you in the shallow end and let you run back and forth, and well, I never told you this Alberta, but Elaine fell in. Tammy, you did too. Just had to do whatever your cousin did. Boots was holding my beer and he grabbed the both of you and put you safely on the grass, then he turned around and went in ass over teakettle himself. You've never seen such a funny thing in your life. He sat there soaking wet and all he could say was 'King, good as new, I never spilled a drop of your beer.' Thought we'd break a rib laughing. You remember, Tammy?"

"No."

"We made a big fire and you made a pig of yourself eating fish."

"I don't remember." I did but I hated this walk down memory lane.

"I remember, Uncle King. I remember. We cooked them

up over an open fire back there, right?"

"That's right, 'Lainy."

"I don't remember," I said. For the longest time I had been searching for a conversation I could hold next to my breast but now that it was here I wasn't going to let him have it. I thought that I had time to hate him like Chan said, but I never had time to make things right because a few minutes later he got a pain in his gut and he gasped for air. Elaine tried to get the oxygen nose plugs back in. Alberta and I stood there useless as tits on a hen. In my mind, I screamed: "I remember, Dad. I thought I forgot but I remember." But no words came.

Years have passed but I just have to say his name and I get a lump in my throat. All I have to do is blink and I'm back there in the good living room, where we sat and waited for death. My mother and I not knowing how to pour him a cup of comfort while Elaine got into bed with death and told it a bedtime story: Tom the Turkey. Dad looked like a little baby as she rubbed his temples and the next thing you know he was purring like a cat. She pulled the covers up around him and gave him a final kiss.

People make their entrances and exits when no one is watching. They cross over in between the slit of the eyelids. When I went out to make us some snacks, he died in her arms.

It's taken years to realize it wasn't personal.

* * * * * *

Death is always a surprise. It's the only thing we know for sure, yet it's always a shock. I knew about paying respects. I had gone to many funerals with J.D. and Nana. They'd stop off at a wake on the way to a picnic or picking up a tractor part. They knew so many dead people. I've seen at least a hundred of them, and it's not as bad as one thinks. Everybody is dressed up smelling like church. There is a sea of white-haired fogies in the receiving line; and when you're little, they just pat you on the head and say, "My, have you ever grown."

That's the other thing that surprises adults. They never expect a kid to grow.

We'd shake hands with the living then kiss the dead. They'd lift me up over the body to kiss the forehead made of stone. Kiss a dead person for good luck. Then we'd eat an egg salad sandwich with the crusts cut off. It wasn't scary, just something we did on the way to somewhere else.

This time death was right there, smirking at me. My father's wake lasted three days. Jack Weiss was the first person I met when I came into the foyer of the Weiss Funeral Home. When he shook my hand and smiled, all I could think of was what King used to say, "If a Weiss is smiling at you, it's not because he's happy. He's just sizing you up."

I entered the viewing room, thinking it would be just family, but there was a real crowd. My brothers and sister were dressed up like it was church time. Elaine stood next to my brother Patrick like she was one of us. Grandma Alice and Grandpa Joe looked lost like they didn't know what to do about a son dead in a box. They were the ones who should've gone first. The aunts and uncles stared ahead – the brothers and their wives. Dad had no sisters. These men had their hands in their pockets and jingled loose change.

The room was full of lilies and church people, whispering politely in the back, and I signed the register book. I could see him lying in the casket from the doorway, laid out with full cheeks. They must've put Kleenex in them because at the end he had a sucked in breath for a face. Now he was looking better than he had in a long time. Someone that healthy-looking shouldn't be lying in a box.

When the people ahead of me cleared the kneeling area, I knelt down in front of the casket and closed my eyes but no prayers came. I knew under the closed half of the box there was a good pair of pants my father would have never worn when he was alive. He wanted to have his work pants on when he went but your wedding and your funeral have nothing to do with you.

"Doesn't he look good?" My mother touched my shoulder.

I wanted to be nice to her. I stood up and gave her a hug but she let out a wail. I thought I'd hurt her. "He was my life," she said, "Lover, oh lover. Lover."

This was a mother I'd never met. The mother I knew did not use the word lover. When she finally unhooked me from her grip, I looked at the faces of my brothers and sister. They were bawling and began holding on to me for dear life. Alberta made room for me in the receiving line and Elaine had the good sense to move, as I was to stand in the position of the oldest.

A moment later, Boots squeezed in next to my mother, and she collapsed into his arms. He said quietly: "It's okay, Alberta. I'm right here."

When they broke apart, Boots reached out and took my hand. I looked up at him. His eyes were so blue it seemed a fish might swim by at any moment. A man that evil shouldn't be good looking, it confuses people. He pulled me in for a hug. I held my breath but he smelled like laundry fresh from the line.

Over the next two days, six hundred people came in and said 'sorry for your loss'.

I was sandwiched in the line between Boots and Alberta. Elaine stood next to her father, their shoulders brushing. We had no time to talk because the people kept coming. Droves of them signed the guest book. Half the county showed up to rubberneck. They came from twenty miles in every direction. He'd fixed a toilet for one, or gave money to another. There were the storeowners to whom he'd delivered ice cream. Then there were the priests, his VON nurse, and the Dairy Princess. They all came, even some of Elaine's customers, nervous people who didn't make eye contact.

My skin was on fire. By the second day of this, I couldn't

take the crowd so I went into the back room. There was no one in there, except Jack. I knew instinctively he'd have booze. I could sniff it out like that. Of course I couldn't ask straight out. I had to go through the charade of making small talk. Small talk is what drunks and funeral directors specialize in. He had the knack of making you feel like you were the only one who lost a person to the authority of death. I talked and squeezed my eyes so I could squeeze out a tear. He pulled out the Tia Maria from his cupboard and poured a shot into a Styrofoam cup. Mission accomplished. After two gulps Jack smiled. The smile you come to know when you look good like me. Men get that look– a dopey dog look like they've been hit over the head with a two by four. Our eyes locked. I hated that it was so easy, so predictable. I hated it. Loved it. That power could create a thunderstorm. I am Eve bringing down all of civilization with one apple.

We didn't do it where he kept the dead bodies. We had sex in a small office with a desk and a file cabinet. The same office where he tried to sell the survivor bigger caskets and waterproof liners. I felt safe in small spaces. Ten minutes of grinding bone on bone. Two people's breath panting back and forth, echo-chugging toward a destination where there is no past, no future. No hurt inside this bag of bones I called body. I had to put my hand over his mouth so he wouldn't make noise. Silence keeps the fire contained. It should have been a one-time thing. But Sundays between four and seven, between the afternoon and evening visitations, I would pick up the phone and he'd be on the other end of the line with his FM radio voice, "You're a very special girl, Tammy." I hated him for his lack of integrity, yet I went back and did it a couple more times to make sure it was as horrible as I first remembered.

At the funeral we were all on display in the front pew. Elaine had loaned me a pair of sunglasses because we got sick of people gawking at us. The ceremony started in the normal fashion with people standing, sitting and kneeling. The Catholics moved automatically into position while Protestants looked around not knowing what to do.

The priest droned on in a hideous voice, the choir sang off key in thin high voices, while the altar boys blessed themselves, thinking they were top bananas for getting the morning off school. Alberta was blatting and bawling and carrying on still after three days. People were getting uncomfortable. I was embarrassed for her. When I went to the can I heard Nana telling the midwife Hester that Alberta was keening like they did in the old country. It's an art form for some; apparently in Ireland you can get hired out professionally. Hester said, "She's not just crying for the dead person but every other sad thing that's happened in her life."

But my mother's bawling seemed to get everybody worked up. In fact, the whole church got into the act. Like yawning, it spread and before you knew it, it seemed they were in the middle of a communal bleat.

It was building to frenzy by the time the priest was shaking the incense over the casket. He was losing control of the crowd so finally he put his hand up and as the church went silent he gestured to a man at the back.

The feet came into focus first. He had forsaken the boots for shoes that squeaked. There was a ledge jutting out of the back of his head; a piece of bone that stood out so far it looked like you could perch a teacup on it. King called that kind of bump the summer kitchen. "They got some summer kitchen hanging off their back porch." That's what he'd had said, if he'd not been so dead.

Boots kept his head down and held his hat in his hands until he passed the front pew. When he genuflected he looked at Elaine and me and nodded a hello and then humbly took his spot at the lectern. At the wake, he'd had a nice sweater on with a good shirt and tie tucked inside his pants. This day he was wearing a suit that looked like he hadn't worn it since high school. Even though he wasn't bloated the way he used to be, it was still too small. The jacket looked like it was going to burst off him. The pants were so short they didn't cover his white socks. He pulled out a long sheet of foolscap paper from his pocket as if he'd been given an assignment to write.

With voice lowered he began, "Mary had a little lamb, her fleece was white as snow."

People shook their heads. Launa and Raju looked at each other and rolled their eyes the way brothers and sisters do. Boots continued, "My English teacher used to tell me that if you're nervous getting up in front of people, quote a nursery rhyme to calm yourself. He cleared his throat and said in too loud a voice, 'MY FEELINGS ABOUT KING BABCOCK', by Stuart Cochrane."

"I'm sure my brother-in-law will go to heaven, but knowing King, he'll have to stop along the way and talk to everyone he knew from Hawley."

The church broke out in laughter. Then he said that King always had such great stories to tell because he listened so carefully to everybody. He spoke of how my Dad could see beyond what people were saying and hear what they really meant. He stopped for a moment, then he lowered his head and said: "I'm alive today because he drove me to the rehab centre. At that point, King's faith in me was the only thing I could pin my hopes on. I know you'll all miss him deeply, especially his kids and Alberta, but if you want to honour King's memory you should know he believed in redemption because he was not just a character, he had character."

He gathered up his papers and walked down the aisle, taking a spot with the men at the back who would normally take up the collection. A eulogy at the best of times is a tale we start to weave once rigor mortis sets in, but this one took the cake. It was a series of well-constructed sentences, strung together by the county's public speech winner.

The reception was back at the farm, and he sat in the

good living room where King had died, and where we wrung our hands over him in the past. A harem of women from the CWL women fawned over him, watching him eat one egg salad sandwich after another. They couldn't fill up his plate fast enough. He sat there like he was Mick Jagger of St. Paul's Church. Funny thing was, he didn't look out of place, holding the fancy china cup, with his pinkie pointing to the ceiling. When he finished eating, he proceeded to ask each and every one of those gathered around him something personal about their lives. For someone who had spent the past two decades in a blackout, he seemed to know everything that was going on in the county. He asked a string of questions of his brothers and sisters, as if while he was lying on that couch pissing himself, he had been keeping one ear to the ground. Did Berle get Tom to plant the herb garden she had been pestering him about? How did Launa fare with the contractor from the reserve? Has he ever come back to finish the cupboards in her kitchen? Did Jinsa finish her doctorate on the effects of transcendental meditation on modern society? It was Biblical: Elaine stared at him like he was Lazarus coming back from the dead.

One father gone. One born again to take his place.

GRIEF

There were train tracks about fifty acres back from our property. At night when the wind was right, you could hear the midnight express blowing through. Elaine and I drove back there often when we were out in the trailer. I remember us sitting in the ditch next to the crossing. We would press our feet up against the side of the embankment to brace ourselves. The force of the train felt like it could pull us under. We'd sit as close as possible, pouring Pixi Stix dust down our gullets, while we counted miles and miles of freight cars heading somewhere we had never heard of. After a hundred cars, counting would bore me. It never seemed to end.

That's what it felt like after my Dad died. I'd think it can't get any worse than this and then another fifty cars would come down the track. The first few days were filled with crying and cooking. There was stuff to tend to but when the casseroles stopped coming and the townspeople went back to their lives, then hopelessness showed up at the door with a suitcase.

Grief arrives between night and day. Around four in the

morning I'd wake up and think the sadness had moved on down the track. For a few moments I'd feel at peace. I'd think: I'm me again but then I would drift up to consciousness and there it was, sitting at the end of the bed, unpacking.

When King died, Alberta was heartbroken but she found it exhausting to be sad. Anger at least gave her some energy. First thing she did was sign up for another winter university course. She'd been chipping away on her bachelor's degree for years, so she signed up for correspondence on Women's Studies. Anyone that entered the barn was asked to drill her on the work of Gloria Steinem and Germaine Greer. Men had done so much to be mad about that she had notes all over the walls of the barn in case she forgot some of their wrongdoings.

"Now they give university courses on how much men have screwed us," Nana said when she sat in the family booth in the China Doll. "They should let me teach it. I could tell them a thing or two."

Nana disapproved of Alberta's behavior. "It's all a way of avoiding reality. She studies late into the night trying to put off having to go in the house and seeing the empty couch."

"Well Nana what do you expect?" I asked.

"I expect not to be feeding a bunch of kids every time I open my door."

"You were at our house for years."

"Don't be sassy. I had nine kids of my own. I'm not raising any more. Poor lambs lost their father. You should stop being selfish. Ccme home and help the little ones." It didn't occur to her I'd lost my father too.

"I don't want to." I snapped. I had to make myself shut down the idea of it or I'd be back there in a heartbeat drowning in all of the work.

"I told your mother to start taking care of those kids. Do you know what she said? I've lost my husband and that's far more painful than anything they're going through."

Nana put out her smoke in the ashtray, shaking her head

and staring hard at me. I reiterated that I was not coming home.

The family kept sending in the troops. The next one sitting in the booth was my brother, Patrick. He came bearing news that Alberta had broken her ribs. As well as fast-tracking her education, the knothead had decided to go to auction to buy some new cattle. When she was trying to push a rowdy heifer down the truck ramp, the thing back kicked her, and broke three of her ribs. Broken ribs are more painful than childbirth. Every time she inhaled it hurt my mother, making it impossible to milk.

"I tried to pitch in but I ain't no good."

"Patrick, stop saying ain't, you sound like an ignorant hillbilly."

"Sorry. Boots came to help for while."

"Boots!" This took the cake.

Although the eulogy was exemplary, I didn't trust his conversion. A public speech is one thing but a leopard doesn't change his spots over night. He seemed to be fooling everybody, taking JD to the sales barn one week and Nana to the track to the next. When he heard Alberta was laid up, he came over, rolled up his sleeves and started helping her milk the herd.

Holding a pillow against her ribcage, Alberta sat on a stool bossing him until he finally exploded, "Alberta you think I never milked a God damn cow." Patrick said it was strange how they acted, teasing each other with stories about how they used to hit and torment each other as children are proned to do. It's hard to think Boots was ever anyone's younger brother. Before you knew it they were doing recitations by Robert Frost and Cremation of Sam Magee by Robert Service: poems they'd memorized from their childhood to suffer through milking time. It might have stayed in the sentimental zone had JD not gotten in on the action. He brought his own stool, trying to escape Nana's bitching. Kids compete when there is a parent there; I don't care how old they are. The two men started pontificating about all the big ideas they'd had before Boots made a mess of his life. Before you knew it, they were planning a comeback; a plan to take the bull by the horns and get the two farms to reflect the reality of the 20th century. The two places could merge and form a co-op and not be giving their profits away in big taxes to the government. If they pooled their resources they could become the county's biggest dairy and beef operation. Boots would be the brawn, and JD would be the brains of the place. Boots only spoke to JD and JD spoke to Boots. They never made eye contact with my mother.

This wouldn't have gone over well at the best of times. Alberta lived for years with a man who offered yards of unsolicited advice. With a belly full of sadness and a mind full of Gloria Steinem it didn't take too many days of this banter before she'd heard enough. She stood up and banged her fist on the barn wall.

"I don't need any suggestions from the likes of the two of you," she roared. A conversion is one thing but telling her how to run her affairs was never going to happen.

"We're just trying to help you out," Boots said as if she should understand this better than anybody.

"Well I don't need your kind of help, do I?"

"Don't be lipping off girl," JD said.

"Yeah, Alberta, 'cam down," Boots said.

"Don't you dare tell me to calm down!"

"I am trying here. Look at me. I've changed."

"Oh really. You were a drunken asshole for most of your life, and now you're a sober one. I don't see much difference."

"I'm just trying to do something normal," Boot repeated in a soft voice.

"See that's the thing Stuart. While you've been sitting over there in pickle juice, "I've been doing normal for decades. Go the hell home."

"Technically, it's my land." JD reminded her.

"All right. You take it back. You want to do the work? Do the work, Dad. Go on. Do it."

As she stormed out, they called her a goddamned feminist so she turned and shook the pitchfork at them. "Don't you dare call me a feminist! I just want things to be fair," which is what all feminists want.

After she told them off, I imagined her lying in bed the next morning, thinking she was free of animals and land.

"King, it's over. No more cattle." I could imagine her reaching across the bed to put her hand on my father's stomach. But only the faint smell of his Old Spice was on the sheets. Grief was the only one there and she hissed at it. Putting the pillow on her ribs to protect her, she pulled on her duds to begin another day. In the light of early morning, I imagine her looking across the fields to the houses where her brother and father lay sleeping, their places still dark with night. Despite giving her resignation, they hadn't listened. They never had. A slight smile crossed her lips. The cows needed to be milked. She could go crazy or not but they were there waiting. Instead of being the curse, there was now comfort with their mind-numbing predictability. She was still Alberta. She was still a farmer.

It was at this time of day I felt we were most connected.

As I lay in bed in town, swatting at the early morning fly buzzing around my head, I would float up to the surface of consciousness. Before the hand of grief pushed me under again, I would remember the salesman and the picture of our farm clipped to a lampshade.

I could almost hear my mother singing, "You've Got to Kiss an Angel Good Morning."

CRAZY

Having people show up at the China Doll asking for Elaine didn't please Chan. He knew she was up to no-good but when I asked him to put me on the prayer list at the church he really started to worry. He begged me to tell him what was going on but I couldn't. Still, I hoped he'd recruit the Catchers and take me away like they had with Lillian and Elaine. Every day there was always one more fire to put out. Gordy became the worry du jour. He was supposed to keep his distance from Elaine. That was the rule: the supplier needed to be far away from the dealer in town. Since this dealer was a girl he showed up on our fire escape on the premise that she'd screwed up the tallies. Elaine didn't make math mistakes. He'd given her two ounces of coke which cost a thousand buck apiece, but he kept insisting it was twenty grand. It was hard to believe an organization like the Hell's Angels wouldn't have brighter people handling their money.

Playing a mathematical doze was code for 'I want to get into your pants. You're bad news" Elaine would scold him which was code for 'I'll let you pop my cherry.'

I wondered how she could fall for such a dumb man. To her, Hell's Angels weren't as bad as their reputation. They were misunderstood boys on bikes.

Snow was the first victim of Gordy's drive-by screwing. He criticized everything she did. The more he put her down, the more she tried to understand him which just made him mad. Finally, exasperated, she said: "Well Gordy if you don't love me anymore, you can just go." She thought that would get him back but those were the words he was seeking.

Off he went to Elaine. Snow thought he was pouting back in Montreal but when she got home and discovered he wasn't there she phoned me in a panic, asking if I'd seen him.

The lovebirds were holed up in the motel on the Trans Canada. I only knew because Gordy constantly complained about the mattress. When I told Elaine I knew what she was doing she acted coy like boffing a Hell's Angel was a sacred act.

Someone who slept with a funeral director has no right to look down on anybody but I knew enough to call what I'd done a fling. She was moon struck. Calling it love is what made it get ugly. Big G insisted they tell Snow because she and Elaine would be working together. Snow was going to continue to provide the delivery service. When they told her, she was stunned. Snow thought the man with twenty woman's names tattooed on his body would never leave her. Sex blinds a person.

Insults were exchanged but no catfight ensued. Snow was too messed up. The whole thing ended with Gordy telling her she could keep the ring. The next night she hawked it, and snorted the proceeds.

After that, I spent a lot of time trying to avoid the lovebirds. Motels are expensive so it seemed every time I walked into the kitchen, I'd find them banging each other up against the counter while the song "Muskrat Love" played on the radio. No matter how many times I cleared my throat to announce my entrance, it never hurried them along. I'd go to the bathroom and turn on the water until they finished.

When I came out, they'd be sitting at the table with no underwear on, bums stuck to our chairs. They'd be wearing matching kimonos he'd gotten them in Montreal's Chinatown. They were identical to the one he'd given Snow. Elaine would ask me to make breakfast for them and all I would think was, "It's a good thing Lillian isn't here." She'd have to hose down the place.

One day the phone rang. When Elaine picked it up, her tone changed completely. She took it into the bedroom for privacy. Gordy started to pace the floor.

"You think it's the narcs, Gordy?" He growled. You didn't do jokes with Gordy. He had no humour glands. When Elaine returned, he was bursting at the seams.

"Who was that, babe?"

"Dad," she said.

When she said the word 'Dad' it was like I'd been punched in the gut. I thought she was talking about King. For a moment I forgot he was dead.

Boots began calling her every day. As I was getting ready for work, he'd ring her up like he'd been doing it for years. I don't know what he was saying, but Elaine began to sound more like a motivational speaker than a daughter. During one of his calls, he must've told her about Alberta running him off because I heard her say, "Dad, you've wasted half your life being looked down on by those people. Now is your chance to prove to them you're not an asshole."

My mother was not my favourite person but I thought Elaine had some nerve criticizing her during her hour of grief.

In short order, Boots joined Gordy sitting at my kitchen table. The only consolation was everyone had underpants on. There they'd sit, discussing the weather. Whether it was going to rain or a drought and what was the almanac predicting. That was the farmer coming out in him. There were so many more interesting things we could've talked about but Boots was blissfully unaware of who or what Gordy was. All he knew was Elaine had a beau. When he discovered Gordy drove a hog, they began to use the word 'torque' a lot. They were getting along well, then the entire thing almost went for a wobbly when Boots started talking about his sponsor and Gordy was nodding his head like he understood. Gordy has a sponsor in the Hell's Angels - a whole other situation. There was no way to clarify it all without opening the can of worms.

"I don't want Gordy to know my dad's an alcoholic," Elaine told me that night. She wanted a father to be proud of so she began hatching a plan to reinvent him. The first item on the agenda was to get the meat shop reopened. The place was run down, with broken refrigerators but they could get it rebuilt if they had the meat orders in place first. J.D could front the cattle costs and she'd get the neighbours to commit to their side of beef before the slaughter so Boots would have the cash up front to renovate.

Gordy and Boots were having a hard time with her reasoning, but then, they didn't have to keep up - they just had to do what she said. It was almost comical to see two such violent men being pussy whipped by a girl.

Gordy seemed enthusiastic at first but one night he called her up and told her his sponsor said he couldn't be associated with her in that way. Screwing her was fine, but when it came to business he had to keep his distance. It was all too dangerous for him. After that call, I had the impression they had broken up, but the next weekend a posse of tattooed guys arrived from Montreal. These were men who owed Gordy a favour.

The men pulled up to Boots' house on their Harley's, a mixed bag of electricians and plumbers, fueled by coke and adrenalin, working day in, day out to create the makeover. They brought new refrigerators and tables from their suppliers. The place was rewired, the shop repainted so that by the time they blew out of town there were no bullet holes, no sign of the past anywhere.

The Shop was named B&E Meats for Boots and Elaine. A photographer from the newspaper came out to take their picture. The next week in the Hawley business section there were Boots and Elaine standing smiling in front of their slogan - "We Know Meat."

CLOSURE

Drunks get born again more than the rest of humanity. They're like cats that way. They have nine lives.

I had managed to keep out of the renovation altogether. Elaine thought I was moping, being a real wet blanket. She expected me to be happy for her but knowing that her good-for-nothing father was alive and mine was dead made me sick. Add the fact that he came by daily for reassurance from everyone, made me want to go looking for a gun. It wasn't good enough he ended up on the front page of the paper, he had to show up at the apartment to crow about it.

That morning I woke up particularly the worse for wear. When he knocked on the fire escape door, I motioned for him to come in but shushed him, because Elaine was still sleeping. He had a pile of newspapers and handed me a copy for my very own.

"Tammy, you should come and see the shop. You wouldn't recognize the place." A ticker tape of venom played inside my head. I didn't trust myself not to make a comeback like: *Oh I bet. Did you take up the shitty piece of wood under the table? Can you go to the bathroom all by yourself now?*

I got off the topic by offering him a tomato juice.

"Hair of the dog?" he asked. "I used to put vodka in my tomato juice every morning with a raw egg," he said, shuddering at me like he couldn't stand to remember.

"I've always loved tomato juice," I replied. I shouldn't have needed to defend my juice choices that early in the morning, especially to the likes of him.

"I like tomato juice, that's all I meant." He smiled in a way that unnerved me, like his brain was boring into mine. He started talking to me about how bad it was when he was drunk and how good it's been since he quit. The monologue was a blur except for the sentence, "I quit drinking. I quit drinking I quit drinking."

Looking back, he was probably thinking out loud. Not thinking about me at all but every time he said 'I quit drinking' a piece of puke came up in my mouth which I swallowed back down. I couldn't drink the tomato juice in front of him because I was afraid he'd think it meant something.

Finally Elaine emerged from the bedroom and they went off to do whatever they had to do but what he said played on my mind all day. By the time I went to the Cadillac, I had nursed his comments into a big grudge.

Backstage, Snow was having another crisis. She had lost all artistic drive after Gordy dumped her. The week before, she had been so out of it she went on stage and that she didn't take a stitch of clothing off. She stood there in the centre of the stage while the men booed her. They hadn't paid attention to her when she was naked but they got deeply offended when they weren't within arm's reach of a tit.

When I had explained to the owner that she was emotionally naked, he told me emotional nudity didn't sell beer. I went back to talk to her and suggested she take a little something off - a glove like Gypsy Rose Lee, something to give them a little titillation - but Snow didn't do anything in half measures. She was a woman of extremes.

The next week she ripped off everything, including the g-string. The farm men booed her again. They wanted mystery not a snatch staring them in the face. Beside, bare snatch was illegal so Frank told me to give her another warning.

"Snow you've got to pull yourself together," You're only hurting yourself."

"I miss Gordy."

"Gordy is going to send you to Parry Sound, if you don't smarten up."

"All I want is closure." She said.

The only closure she was going to get was broken bones or a shot in the head. I wiped the coke booger from her nose and showed her the newspaper of Boots and Elaine.

"See this. This is as close to closure as anyone ever gets." I touched the photo of Boots and Elaine.

"She's a douche bag." Snow sniffed at me. "*They* managed to get closure. They've rewritten it all, wrapped it up and put a bow on it. But we don't get a bow, we don't get a bow." Snow snorted another line. I drank another drink. The more she snorted, the more I drank and the more we talked to ourselves. Every few seconds she'd say, 'damn douche bag'. There we sat for hours having two conversations that neither one of us was listening to.

"He has some nerve."

"Like a canal horse pushing back in people's lives.'

"Does what he like when he likes."

"Never any regard for anyone but himself."

"That's what he does. He's forgets what he has done,"

"He'll forget me."

"He'll forget dad, Reg. Poor Reg. Did he deserve that guy's craziness? No. The dog was innocent."

"I was innocent."

"I told myself I'd never forget him."

"Everybody forgets. I wrote Karen Kain. She didn't write back."

"Screw Karen Kain."

"Yep. They move on. Everybody forgets."

"Not me," I said. "Not me." I said it again. I had one of those ideas that sounded very intelligent at two in the morning. "Not me, Snow."

"What?" Snow asked. Her nostrils were bleeding.

"We're going to show him what hair of the dog really is." I left her there, drawing a moustache on Elaine's photo with an eyebrow pencil, and ran out front. The bar was closed for the night but Blacky was on his regular bar stool. I begged him to drive me out to the farm. He'd lost his license years ago so it took us nearly an hour to go seven miles because he had to take the back roads to avoid the cops.

When we turned down our side road, I had him park about a half mile from the farm. I left him dozing while I headed to the field behind Boots' house.

It was pitch black, a moonless night, but my feet knew where they were going. I scurried to the edge of the property line that divided his place from ours. The only sound was the hydro poles humming as I came to stand at the burial place. The clay was stubborn so I broke my beer bottle and clawed out scoops of earth with the jagged edge. We had dug only a shallow grave, so the dog's skeleton was a few inches beneath the surface. Skeleton is not quite the right word for what was left. It was just a pile of bones. No maggots or flies. The hide was stripped off by weather and decomposition and there were patches of fur in the bottom of the hole. I held up the skull and examined it for bullet holes but there was no evidence of violence. Just a dead dog reduced to a pile of bones.

I should've left it, but there was a drunken rage coursing through me. Reg needed to be vindicated even though the only thing I remembered about the mangy piece of shit was that he barked every time a leaf blew across the driveway.

I took the skull and walked across the field to Boots' doorstep. I laid it on the stoop, and ran like hell back to the car as if I was in a twisted game of Nicky-Nicky nine door.

When I woke the next morning, everything came back in Technicolour.

You dug up a dog last night. There is no hiding. You are dead. Run.

I tried to get up but there was an arm on my stomach, holding me down. When I looked over, there was Blacky, snoring to beat the band. A dead dog and a pickled old egg, farting beside me. I walked out to the kitchen. Gordy and Elaine were banging each other. Muskrat Love was playing, as the phone began to ring. It was eleven o'clock.

Suddenly my thoughts cleared and I saw my future. If I stayed there one minute more I would die. In my nightgown I ran downstairs to the restaurant and asked Chan to take me to the Furlong Hospital where they put drunks and people with bad skin.

ADMISSION

Chan didn't ask any questions, he just got out the car and drove me to the hospital. When we walked into Emergency, he talked to the receptionist.

"This not normal girl. I buy placemats and she drink half the alphabet. Liquor license bad luck. No alcohol in China Doll though any more. New Chan Rule."

"Okay sir I need you to calm down."

"She and cousin shouldn't be together. She always try be like Elaine. Elaine not notice. Just like Dolly and me."

"Okay, thank you. Just take a seat. I'll call Psych and get her assessed." After a small eternity a tight-lipped psych resident emerged from the on-call room.

My feet were bleeding. I was sitting there in my nightgown. She asked, "Does anyone in your family find you acting strange?" I stared at her.

"She drink like fish." Chan said, but no one listens to anyone with an accent.

"Are you a threat to yourself or others?"

"Yes, I dug up Reg."

"You said that but I find it hard to believe you would have the strength to do that."

"He was only 15 pounds.'

"But you said he was seven." She looked at her notes, confused.

"Reg was a dog."

"What? You dug up a dog?" She scratched her bed head hair.

"I dug up a dog and put in it on Boots' doorstep. He got admitted years ago because he killed that same dog. Of course he never got charged."

"You think Boots remember dog. He don't remember dog," Chan piped in.

"Please sir, go over there and sit down in the waiting room." The resident pointed to an empty red bucket chair. As Chan was taking his seat, he threw another comment our way.

"I just say you put bones on his doorstep – You think Boots will know those bones belong to Reg? He will think cat brought bones and put on doorstep as a prize."

"Sir, please."

"Bones?" Chan muttered as he plunked himself on the chair. "What kind of big statement is that, Tamara?"

"All right, I heard you." I yelled back at him and turned to her." Digging up a dog is not normal right? Snow started talking about closure and that's when I got the idea."

"This Snow is the stripper with two vaginas? I've never heard of this condition. How do you know she had two vaginas?

"Ask Gordy. He was sleeping with her." I sniffed.

"Okay I am confused. I thought he was sleeping with Elaine?"

"Before. He was sleeping with her before."

"Tell me more about Elaine."

"It's not about her. Okay? It's about me. I dug up a dog. That should be enough."

"Do you hear voices?"

"Yes, but never from people I want to hear from. My father won't say a damn thing to me though one time I think I felt him hovering there when I was peeing."

"Your father watched you when you pee?" She started writing very quickly.

"No from heaven. When I go to the bathroom I feel him there, so I keep the lights off, because it freaks me out."

"Oh he's dead. He died when?"

"A few months ago."

"I see. I am sorry." Her tone got softer.

"Thanks."

"I mean that's stressful. He was young, then?"

"Just forty."

This sleepy resident reached out and touched my hand.

"Hi, I'm Reen." Suddenly because I said I had a dead father, I'd become a human being. Tears were running down my cheeks and I didn't know why. Honesty poured out of me from somewhere. "It has been like sleeping with the lights on. When I wake up all that pain is sitting at the end of the bed, smoking a Peter Jackson. You know some people picture themselves with a future, when I look in the mirror I can't see my face beyond this point."

"So you're suicidal?

"No. I just don't think I can keep living."

"Why don't we admit you and you see if you can get you some rest."

The psych ward wasn't as peaceful as I thought it would be. There was always someone who was crying. Nurses came with apple juice spiked with nothing. I was hooked up to an IV to that kept me in a slow-release Valium fog. Every time I came to, there was somebody standing over me: Alberta with her rosary beads, Nana telling me I was getting fat, some schizo chick doing my hair in a lovely French braid. For the next few days I drifted in and out of consciousness.

When I came to I think it was night, as my supper tray is still there. Elaine was sitting at the end of the bed, eating my pudding.

"So you're doing okay?" She moved toward me to give me a drink.

"Oh I'm fine." I sipped water from a bendable straw. "I am suffering from nervous exhaustion."

"Is that what they're calling it?"

"Oh, they think maybe it's a break down. They are some specialists looking into it." I smiled feebly. Out of the blue, she asked: "So, why did you put a dead dog on our doorstep?" Just like that. No delay. No building up to it. Just accusation.

"What? A dead dog?" My mouth hung open in mock shock.

"You know damn well what I'm talking about. He practically tripped over it when he went out for the newspaper that morning."

"A dog? There was a dog? Well why would anybody...well that's strange." I was shaking.

"Boots saw the bones. He started to shake. I was terrified that he was going to go off the deep end. I called the guys from the double A's and they drove him around most of the afternoon. The one thing I didn't forgive myself for, you go and rub it in my face."

"Honest to God, I didn't dig up any dog." I said.

"God, now you're going to lie. That's a surprise."

"I'm not lying. Honest to God."

"If he drinks because of this you won't be in the nuts ward. You'll be in the cemetery. I'll get Gordy to break every bone in your body."

"Gordy touches me and he'll go to jail."

"And so would you."

"What? I haven't done anything."

"You think you're innocent? Gordy would rat you out as soon as look at you. You think he wouldn't?"

"Yeah well, nice boyfriend you have there."

"You jealous? I've got somebody. You don't."

"Jealous? What is there to be jealous about?"

"It must be hard always looking down from your throne, eh Tammy? Sitting on the sidelines, acting like you know better than everybody."

"I'm tired and I am...." I went to ring for the nurse but when I pushed the button it didn't do anything.

"You can't stand that I keep moving forward. So you sneak around and do shit always in a backhanded way. You just can't be honest. You could never ever be honest."

"I didn't do anything to the dog."

"Yeah right. When you get out of here, don't bother coming back to the apartment. We are done. You and I are done."

"I didn't do anything, honest to God! Please Elaine, please." I tried to sit up but I was too drugged up for my legs to move. She turned around and walked out.

The next day when Chan came in, I told him I wouldn't be living in the apartment any more.

"Elaine has no say in your life."

"Chan I can't go back. She knows everything. She's never going to forgive me."

"She know nothing. Elaine never come here to talk to you last night. Must be big dream you have. She arrested two hours after you get admitted. Someone call cops. She in jail and she won't be out for long time."

EPIPHANY

A lot of ghosts like to give parting words of wisdom before they move on. Hearing a few last words from a dead person is generally acceptable, I've found. But I had an imaginary conversation with a live one.

Alberta thought this was another stunt. She sat at the end of my bed and told me I had better get into reality pretty damn quickly, or I'd end up in the detention centre like Elaine. She slapped the newspaper in front of me and there on the front page was the story about the big drug bust. Elaine's mug shot looked sexy. It said, 'Hawley Police bust up alleged drug ring. Acting on an anonymous tip, police charged Elaine Cochrane with drug possession with intent to sell. Captain John Dafoe wouldn't disclose the amount seized but Miss Cochrane is being held without bail.' Snow got her closure.

"Was Elaine the only one who got busted?" I wondered if Gordy had been arrested too, but Alberta thought I was talking about myself.

"Yes, just her. You're damn lucky."

Yes, Alberta, I'm a lucky girl. I'm in a psych ward. I see

people that aren't there. I dug up a dog because I have a dead father. Why, I have a horseshoe up my ass.

"So, what is going to happen to her?" I asked.

"Boots has a lawyer helping her. He's frantic. You two. I knew this wasn't right. I could feel it in my bones that the two of you were up to no good. Were you doing drugs, Tammy? Is this why you're acting like this?"

"No I wasn't."

"Well, I don't believe it." She stared into my eyes to will a confession out of me.

"I wasn't."

"Well Chan and the boys from the bar all said you had nothing to do with any of it. If I hadn't been praying it would've been you in there right along with her."

"Were you praying for Elaine?" I asked.

"Of course I was. I pray for everybody in the god-forsaken country. "

She didn't think I was experiencing a weird psychotic break. To her this was all in my head. It was in my head, but not in a manic depressive, schizophrenic kind of way. Just in a boring, neurotic kind of way. She must have been scared because she encouraged me to speak to Dr. Reen St. Clair, the resident who had admitted me. For once I agreed with Alberta. I wanted to see the shrink. While other patients licked white glue from the palm of their hands during craft time, I went to her office to talk.

I'd imagined I would lie on a couch and smoke but I had to sit across from her, eyeball to eyeball. It felt like confession. I recited my sins over and over, hoping for absolution. 'I dug up the dog. I imagined a conversation with Elaine. I am nuts. I'm bad.' Give me three Hail Mary's so I can move on.

That wasn't good enough for Reen. She wanted me to talk about why I dug up the dog. What was I feeling before I did it? I was feeling drunk was what I wanted to say. I didn't know why I did what I did. I didn't know me at all. If I had died in the chair talking to Reen it would've been Elaine's life that flashed before my eyes.

One part of me wanted help. The other part thought it was all bullshit. Her shrink logic made my head ache:

"Perhaps Elaine speaking to you was some kind of transference,"

"You mean it was a guilty conscience?"

"Yes, but it's rather ironic that you lied to Elaine about the digging up the dog."

"She'd have killed me if I told her the truth."

"But she wasn't there. You dug up the dog and you lied to yourself about it."

She waited a few minutes but as I didn't say anything else she told me to go back to my room and think about it. I thought and thought and the next time we had a session I'd come up with a good answer.

"Well, what I came up with sounds stupid," I said.

"Nothing is off limits."

"I think God was talking to me," I said.

"God?" By the look on her face I could tell this was not the answer she was hoping for. She looked like she was about to call a code.

"I've been very religious and well I might have been in the middle of an epiphany."

"An epiphany? Tell me about this 'epiphany' idea."

"Well, there was a moment of clarity where God opened up the curtain of life and let me see inside my own head. That conversation was the most honest conversation we never had."

"Right, but God didn't appear. Elaine did. Is Elaine God?

"No. God is God. But I wouldn't listen to him, because I don't believe in him and he knows that, so he got my attention by appearing as Elaine." Epiphanies are a lot like telling someone your dreams. They lose something in the translation.

"I don't understand what God has to do with this. On

your chart it says you're a Buddhist."

"Well no, but I know one. I am a pseudo Buddhist. It might not have been God, but it was definitely a voice inside of me."

"I would call that your conscience."

"Okay have it your way." People tell you to be honest and they argue semantics.

"No it's not my way. It's your way Tammy. You have to find your way. You have to stop agreeing with me."

"Okay."

"You have to stop holding onto something outside yourself. Like God or Elaine. You have to start knowing what you think so you can develop coping strategies."

"All right."

"Well, so what did your conscience tell you?"

"It told me that I could never be the craziest one in the room, can I? I will always be out-done by her."

"It's a competition then?"

"No. But no matter how bad my life gets, hers will always be worse."

"You're in a Psych ward," she asked.

"I will never ever be able to out-crazy the crazy."

Reen didn't understand my thesis. She didn't have much faith in my epiphanies or any of my insights. She didn't believe in grand gestures from the universe. For her, life was a series of choices. "You choose."

Finally I told her I was sick of not 'choosing' right. That I was only seventeen and she should just let me believe what I wanted to believe.

She signed a release form and shook her head. She must have been expecting failure because she gave me a list of rules; a series of techniques for choosing sanity. I had to exercise. And breathe. Apparently I'd been breathing wrong my entire life.

The only thing we agreed on was that I had to steer clear

of Elaine. So everybody got on board. Chan moved my stuff out of the apartment and into Dolly's room at Chan's. He worked it out so that I only had lunch shifts. I could be done before the Cadillac Tavern would be a temptation.

But, I couldn't escape the story. The town of Hawley hadn't seen that kind of action in years. People were chewing away on it for weeks, shaking their heads and not understanding how drugs had found their way into their town. They sighed in my direction and said, 'Thank the Lord that the riff raff has been taken care of. I would've locked up your cousin and thrown away the key.'

I listened in on them discussing how the trafficking charges had been dropped but Elaine was going have to serve time for possession. Two years minus a day was a provincial sentence which meant she was supposed to be in with less hardened criminals. Less hardened compared to what? Was she going to have the top bunk? The lower one? She needed air. She wouldn't do well without exercise. She'd get hyper and drive everybody nuts and then somebody would stab her. I knew that she would have a hard time being in confinement. Every single minute of every single day she was all I could think of.

I thought I would feel better if I could just see her one more time. Just one more time and then I'd let her go. I asked Chan if he would take me to her on Visitor's Day but he would not. He and the guys at the Cadillac Tavern had successfully convinced the police that I had nothing to do with any of it. They didn't want me to draw attention to myself but I had been with her my whole life. Not going to her was far more suspicious, but Chan would have no part of it.

The ache was unbearable. The epiphany was fading. I couldn't remember what my big insight meant. So finally I went into the Cadillac to see what the men could tell me. I could thank them for covering for me. Blacky was at the bar but when I sat down he got up and began playing darts. I tried to order my usual but Frank refused to serve me. "You have I.D.? No? Well you're a minor. We don't need any more trouble."

After he escorted me to the front door, my appreciation for getting off the hook waned. Nobody was going to tell me what I could or couldn't do. Nobody ignores me. I went to the LCBO and drank a bottle of vodka, on their front step. By the end of the night I was screaming at the closed door of the bar. "Blacky you were damn lucky to have a sexy girl like me!"

By night's end I was on that gurney again, swearing at Reen for not rearranging my thoughts in the right order. We made another list. And another. For the next fourteen months it was like a revolving door. The episodes came, sometimes with a whimper, sometimes with a bang, but the turn around time from being in the hospital to being out of was faster and faster.

There was certain predictability in madness. A momentary relief, followed by numbness. There was Valium and do-gooders. Those folks would arrive with A Line skirts and dour faces like crumpled Kleenex.

"Why? Tammy Why," they'd ask. And I'd offer all the reasons Reen had created for me.

"I was born with psoriasis. I am thin-skinned. I have a Third Eye. I'm a Catholic. I'm delusional. I have low impulse control. I am the oldest. My father died. My mother's too hard on me. Nana ran away from home. They worked me to death."

Pick a card, any card. There were a million reasons but knowing them didn't change anything. I had become the charity case; their fifteen-minute Sunday afternoon visit. Now I knew how Grandpa Joe felt.

Every Sunday, we'd go to the nursing home and pepper him with questions, wanting to milk some nugget of information from him. "What's happened, Grandpa?" Nothing is what happened. From one end of the week to the next he sat there, hour after hour, doing nothing, being spoon-fed; having his ass wiped by someone he didn't know. 'Smile, Grandpa, smile.' What did he have to smile about? Those visits were endless, the longest fifteen minutes of the week because everybody was trying too hard.

When I look back, I still don't know why I acted the way I did. The only thing I know for sure is the Psych wards are full of people who've had epiphanies. Crazy people have them as often as they change their socks. The problem is, nobody tells them how to cope after they have the brilliant aha, when life returns to normal and things go disappointingly gray. Even saints for all their blinding insights never gave instructions on how to cope with life. Not one of them wrote a book called "The Day After the Epiphany". That is because saints for the most part were dull villagers who thought it was good enough that God gave them any relief at all.

ALICE

Protestants aren't as prone as Catholics to flashes of insight. They were more content with patient improvement.

I found out this when I went to stay with Grandma Alice. Since Grampa Joe was in the nursing home, she asked if I'd like to come and stay with her a bit. She was lonely, she said. If I helped her out she told me she'd give me room and board.

Living in town wasn't working for me. People blamed it on the urban setting and thought country air would help. Alberta had made some feeble suggestion to have me move back home, but she didn't want that any more than I did. Once you leave home you can't live under the same roof with your mother. As much as she didn't want me coming back, she got herself into a flap about me moving over to that side of the river.

"Alice doesn't wear underpants."

"Why are you telling me this Mother?" I thought she'd be happy somebody was taking me off her hands.

"I'm just saying she doesn't know enough to keep her drawers on." Alberta was basing this on some story she'd heard from JD. Apparently thirty years ago he was dropping off some cattle to Grandpa Joe. When he was unloading them off the back of the truck, he caught Grandma Alice peeing by the rose bush. He went around telling everybody that would listen that she didn't wear underpants. That was a terrible rumor to start about her. If she wasn't wearing underwear, it was because she had a terribly big rear end, and it was likely hard to find something to fit her. As for peeing outside, I don't know why he would've cared. It didn't hurt the roses any. They grew like weeds all over the south side of the house. But as I say, it takes family a long time to change their minds about you. It takes years before they'll update their files.

Alice was poor. They lived in squalor but she had a kindness my mother's family didn't know. Even though her heart had been broken a hundred times in life she didn't go into the negative.

I went back and forth to the hospital, like a revolving door, but she never judged me for it; never judged my confusion.

"I don't know why I do what I do. I am destined to be crazy." I hoped she might tell shed some light on it.

"You're lucky though, getting help at your age. Some people live a lifetime and don't know they're not right in the head," she'd say. Then she'd cut the hospital bracelet off my wrist and get the flour out to make bread. Something about cooking always made me hopeful, especially baking bread in a wood stove like she did. You had to watch it, carefully. If you didn't control the heat it would be raw in the middle and burnt on the bottom.

Alice knew how to cook, the way a fat woman usually does. She'd knead the dough into mini loaves. It was nothing for her to make ten loaves a day. We'd take it out of the oven and eat slice after slice slathered in butter, dipping each piece in the canned peaches she'd done up the year before; we nearly choked on the sweetness of the syrup.

Over those months in and out of the hospital, I'd come back to her like a mangled tomcat. She'd clean me up. We'd sit at that table, her telling me stories about my father. Enough time had passed that I could hear about him without feeling bad.

"He had a screw loose too. Once when he was fourteen, I asked him to shovel snow out the driveway. When I looked out, he had made circles, creating patterns like snowflakes with his shovel. Nobody could've ever found our front door. I was some mad, so he hid in the barn the entire night. I had to get Joe to take supper out to him. I never appreciated that he could see things that no one else could."

"He never saw me."

"He bragged about you all the time. Tammy this. Tammy that. He was always talking about the one he wasn't with. King tried too hard to make everybody like him. All the joking he did, but there was a terrible sadness following him from the time he was a teenager." She said this like it was nothing to be ashamed of.

"He had sadness?"

"Sure couldn't you could feel it coming off him?" Alice validated what I knew on some level my whole life. My intuition was right. I did sense the sadness in my father. She continued,

"He got sad after the fever. See when he was a teenager our whole family came down with Scarlet Fever. It's not much of an illness to fight these days but back then the weak and infirm were taken out."

"King was the only one who didn't catch it because he had been haying down the road for days at the Clements. But all us ones still living at home came down with it, including Pansy, who was only four years old."

"Who was Pansy? I asked.

"My baby girl."

"I didn't know there was a Pansy," said I. He never told

us anything about his side of the family.

"Pansy was a whip of a thing and didn't have the strength to fight it when it came. She passed in the middle of the night. I wasn't allowed out to go to my own baby girl's funeral. The arrangements were left to King. He had to buy a dress for her down at the Sell Rite and pass it through the window. They dressed her and passed her body in the coffin out through the window and the funeral director took her to be buried. King was the only one standing there at the graveyard as they lowered her into the ground. I always thought he never got over that she died and he lived. He thought about things way too much. You're just like him, with all that thinking."

"I can't help the ideas I have Grandma." I felt I had to defend myself.

"I know doll, no one can help how their head works. But some ideas just plumb wear a person out. At least that's what I've found. When Pansy died, my idea was that I would never be happy again ... and thought my heart was broke and I thought that was it. But before you knew it, Doug my youngest was born. God that child made me laugh and well you can't be sad all the time when you have babies."

"You don't know it when you're as young as you, but life has a way of taking something away and then dropping something down to take its place," Alice said.

"Your Daddy found your mother two weeks after he buried Pansy. God took my Joe to town to the nursing home and took your Dad in the same year. And once again I was thinking I won't be able to handle it out here, then I got the idea for you to come. What a gift."

"I'd hardly call it a gift." I laughed.

"I got what I asked for. My head told me you wouldn't come. My head said your mother wouldn't let you. But I didn't listen to my head. I went and asked you anyway."

She stuck two slices of bread in her pocket and waddled

up to bed. I looked out the small dirty window of the house where he grew up.

With the wind blowing dead weeds across the field I realized my head had been holding me hostage. I thought because I was insightful on some accounts, that I should've been able to forecast outcomes ahead of time. I should've not told him off. When he said, 'There's your version of things and my version of things and then there's the truth." I should've known that it really meant he was sick and dying and wanted me to come back before he died.

But how could I have known that? I was too busy being mad that I wasn't his favourite; that King was public property and never rose up to save me.

There was too much chaos blowing around me to know what to listen to and what to ignore. And now he was dead and back in heaven with Pansy, another girl who needed him.

"I am sorry I was difficult." I wasn't groveling when I issued the words.

"Forget about it Tammy. You're a teenager. Teenagers don't know shit."

It wasn't his voice. It was my own. There was nothing sentimental about any of it, but things started to inch forward.

TREATMENT

When we were in Grade six we had a teacher who had B.O. Mr. Munds stunk to high heaven. At recess Elaine and I were imitating him, and when he caught us I denied it flatly, said I was talking about somebody else. But she stood there and coughed up the truth.

"Yes I was mocking you," she looked straight ahead with eyes twitching.

"Do you realize that you hurt my feelings?"

"Do you realize your stink hurts mine?" He dragged her off to the principal's office. She got the strap, which in those days was a lot like the death penalty. Not many girls were given it. The principal wanted to make an example of her so he bought her in and placed her at the front of the class. I sat safe at the back with my head bent down. She held out her hand as the rest of the class watched. She stood there not flinching, staring at the wall. She didn't cry. She didn't pull her hand back.

When she went to jail, it was the same. She took the hit for everybody. Her suppliers were what they were looking for, not some seventeen-year old, but she did a lot more time than she should have because she refused to tattle. Elaine wasn't a criminal compared to the ones in there. Instead of being the worst person in the room she was the best. She studied and got good marks so they let her take some university courses. For once in her life she had some structure and she did well with it. At least that was the story.

Maybe neither one of us had an epiphany. But something was changing for both us. I dug up the dog; there was no turning back. No going back to the good old days. We were both being pushed forward in different directions.

I stopped drinking. Not once in any of my admissions to the hospital did anyone ask me if I drank too much. Chan must've said it a hundred times during those months of being admitted. One day after my shift I sat befuddled and said to Chan,

"If I'd lived in Victorian times I would've ended up as one of those insane aunts they put up in the attic to hide from being seen when company came. Those batty women you read about in storybooks covered in lace and spider webs. What is that pounding on the ceiling? Oh that? That's just the crazy Aunt Tammy. Crazy Third- Eyed Tamara. "

"You not crazy! You like Dolly. You can't handle booze." I was shocked. Not by the idea that Dolly drank. That actually explained some reason for her awful disposition. I was surprised he was telling me I couldn't handle it.

The penny dropped.

It should've been obvious. I had been drinking almost daily since I was fourteen. But no one ever said it. No therapist. No doctor. I agreed to go to a treatment centre near Furlong. In fact I went twice. The first time I got kicked out for drinking. After fourteen days of those endless AV presentations on how my liver functioned I was bored stiff.

Look at my liver. I've got cirrhosis. What the hell! Let's go for a cocktail.

The second time, it took but I came back pregnant. Day fourteen was the transition day again. I got bored. Had an itch. I got together with a coke addict named Tom. I didn't get his last name, just his initial. Tom B. was the father of my baby. An anonymous sperm donor.

I don't understand why some kids are conceived and some aren't. There is no logic to any of it. I had been on birth control but this time it didn't work. I didn't want a kid. I didn't want to have anybody's baby, ever. It seemed like I'd raised a family myself. When I came back home, I knew something wasn't right. I had puked so many mornings drinking I guess it didn't register for awhile. By three months it was obvious so I took a test.

I was still seeing Reen for weekly sessions. When I told her about the pending bundle of joy, she told me I was choosing, which was so unhelpful. She was useless but having a bad shrink is better than having no shrink. I didn't know what to do so in desperation I told Alberta the truth for the first time ever. I just said it. I didn't make excuses. I didn't sugar coat it. Nothing. And she did what Alberta did. She said, 'You have to do everything the hard way don't you Tammy?'

Instead of arguing with her I agreed. I do have to do things the hard way. As per usual she and Nana sat around and bitched about me - then they bought wool to knit booties. When my water broke the bunch of them came cross the river ready for action.

The baby was three weeks late. I was as big as a barn. I was lying on Alice's couch. She had put plastic sheets down and was wearing her Wellingtons. When she heard their truck pull up she looked out the dirty window and said, "The cavalry has arrived."

They didn't bother to knock, just burst in on us with a pile of instruments, and started sterilizing the place. Alice took no offense that she wasn't clean enough for them.

"God Tammy. You held off did you?" Like anyone can

hold off the force of nature.

"You took long **enough**." I screamed as the next contraction doubled me.

"If you lived closer we could have made it before now." It was only seven miles start to finish, but living on that side of the water you'd think she had to cross the border.

"Did you drink warm milk and onions?" the old one with the wig asked.

"Shit no. That would make me sick."

"Tammy, don't swear." Alberta will be bossing me until her dying day. She had worn King's sweater so that when she bent down to kiss me I could smell him again.

"Mary please put out that cigarette." Hester popped her head up from between my legs. The one who delivered all of Nana's kids wouldn't miss delivering another generation.

"It helps me focus," said Nana.

"I mean it Mary. Put your smoke out." Nana butted her smoke in the can of sand Alice had near the stove.

"It's different when you see your own child having a child." Alberta said. "I just don't know why you won't go to the hospital."

"Mother. I want natural."

"There's nothing noble about natural." How her tuned had changed since my birth. But after five kids I guess she had the right. We're all filled with good intentions until the first contraction comes then its damn the torpedoes and every woman for herself.

"She's got a ways to go," said Hester.

The pain ebbed and flowed for the next twelve hours. In the middle of the night it stopped altogether. The women passed the waiting time by gossiping.

"How's Boots' girl doing?" Hester asked.

"She's out now, living up in Furlong, going to school. See the good part of being rehabilitated is she got out she got her education free." Alberta kept in touch with her on and off.

"Free? Well that's nice," Hester said.

"Yeah criminals and the military get everything in this country," Nana said.

"You know what she told me" Alberta asked? "She was the one who called the cops."

"What?" I sat up. "Why would she do that?"

"She called the cops on herself?" Alice asked. "That don't make any sense."

"That doesn't make sense." I said. I wasn't correcting Alice's language I was actually agreeing with her.

"She said it. Not me," said Alberta.

"I don't believe it," I said.

"The words came out of her own mouth. She said it was getting crazier by the minute and well she was tangled up with a bad bunch of apples. The Hell's Angels."

"The Hell's Angels?"

"Well that's what she said. I read an article in MacLean's and well those Hell's Angels are very violent."

"Are they now?" asked Alice.

"Yes, and I'm not endorsing the drug culture at all but she would never have gotten ahead in a male dominated organization like that. They are very sexist."

"I don't want to hear about Elaine." I muttered.

"I'm just making small talk."

"I can't hear about her, okay?" It wasn't jealousy this time. It was far more than that. They didn't understand that one of the things that helped me stop drinking was if I didn't think about her. If I spoke about her at all, it started the ache in me again. A phantom pain would shoot through me and I'd want to drink.

"No more Elaine or I won't be able to do this okay?" I pointed to my stomach.

"Okay."

"I mean it. She can't be talked about in my presence."

"All right. All right I am sorry. Okay." I knew Alberta

didn't get this. And she didn't have to. If I was going to do have a new life, I had to expunge the word Elaine from my life. There wasn't room for her in my head.

Alberta held my hand as I pushed down.

"Ahhhhhh Mommmm I'm in so much pain."

"I know Tammy, I know."

"I think I'm dying."

"I know I know." I looked into my mother's eyes and when she said ' I know'

I knew she did.

"The head is crowning," Hester cried.

"I can't look, I can't look," said Alberta.

"Give her one more good push Tammy." Hester pushed on my gut.

One final push, a final bear down. The old mid-wife maneuvered the head and out he came.

"You got a boy."

"A boy?"

Hester cut the cord and put him on my stomach. I had a boy. A small wee thing with a scrunched up head that looked like it would never straighten out. Nana washed him off and they all took a turn, cooing and smelling his fresh baby smell. It was Alberta, kissing him that touched me the most. As she held Daniel, he wiggled and scrunched up his face like an old man. My mother nestled that small head to her neck and it was like meeting myself for the first time.

MARKET

I was spoon fed normal until I got a taste for it. After Daniel was born, Alice moved into town into the same nursing home as Grandpa Joe. Even though he didn't know her, she wanted to be around in case he had a moment of lucidity.

"You can't leave me. I don't know what I'm doing," I said.

"You'll figure it out." She hugged me and told me I could stay as long as I needed.

Beggars can't be choosers, but it was a tough slog out there. She had electricity but the well went dry more times than I could count. When we did have water I was using a ringer washer feeding each diaper through until my arm wanted to fall off.

I told people in town I was living the life of a hippie out there by myself. But the days were endless, and nights were longer.

When Alice lived there, we both slept up in the upstairs bedrooms even though they weren't insulated. It was during my foggy days when I hadn't noticed how cold it was. After

Daniel was born, I'd wake up in the morning and he'd be under the covers, nestled in under my armpit, the heat pouring out of him. I'd be soaked with sweat and then start to shiver. The first thing I did was to drag the bed and crib down to the good living room, so we could hole up close to the stove. We cooked, ate and slept in there.

Nights out there, I almost lost my mind with the baby crying. I was only twenty-two. I loved him plenty. But there was no man. No heat. No sleep. It's a wonder I didn't throw one of us out the window. It was brutal but Alice was right. Alongside the pain runs another runs electric current of joy.

******

Grandma Alice had stocked the freezers with bread and soup before she headed off. Alberta gave me all her vegetables and fruit. Boots to give me a side of beef before he closed the meat shop for good. After the Elaine incident he was too full of shame to live in the public eye.

Nothing like despair to get you motivated to change something. I had managed to graduate high school. Drunk, I still got honours. I had tried going to college but between teenage hormones and baby hormones there were no brain cells left for focusing. Not that I wasn't a good worker. I did odd jobs here and there but nothing I could call an occupation.

It was in early spring that l looked in the freezer and saw the last of the food. I decided to take some of my baking to market. I didn't have money enough to even begin the baking production so I borrowed some from Alberta. Her wallet doesn't open wide for many but she knew I could cook. I had to get a vendor's permit and when the market opened the last Saturday in May, there we were; me on my lawn chair and Daniel in the stroller, sitting in the middle of the Town Square in Hawley.

The pies and breads always went first. After a couple of

weeks, people were there waiting in line by seven-thirty. I'd be tempted to pack up the squares and go home right after the first rush. I was worried that I'd run into some of the old crowd. Then I realized the folks from the Cadillac Tavern weren't up at that time of day. So as I got more used to things, I began to hang around longer for socializing as much as anything. It was good to be out talking to grown-ups one day a week.

I met so many people. There was one woman my age selling her own honey as well as some jewelry she designed. Her name was Hilary and over the weeks we struck up quite a friendship. She was the same age as I was, and had two babies close to the same age as Daniel. We talked while the kids and customers kept us hopping. For the first time in my life I had a friend who wasn't a relative.

Saturday started becoming my favorite day of the week again. I started going earlier than the others to put on a pot of coffee for everyone setting up. I'd slice up a loaf of my baked bread so the other vendors would have a little something to eat. The ones who'd gone to market for decades were suspicious of my generosity, thinking I was going to take over their stalls or get too big for my britches. I don't know what they were worried about. I had no time for a coup. Baby care, baking and maintaining sanity was a full time job. I'd come home after a day like that and drop into bed.

Despite the fatigue I started feeling like a respectable citizen. My mind felt well, too. I wasn't measuring how much I'd changed. I knew something had shifted when I saw Boots again. He was living in an apartment house on Water Street on the other side of town. We had seen each other at a family function or two over those last couple of years. After I'd been to treatment he seemed to have a soft spot for me. Despite the need some recovering booze-hounds have to apologize, I didn't say a thing to him about digging up the dog. He never mentioned it - if he knew. If he didn't know it would've served no good purpose to bring it up except to alleviate my guilty conscience. He had killed the dog. I had dug it up. We were even.

I had made my peace with him in my head. He was in a neutral zone. Still he seemed to think he and I were old buddies or something. He'd show up at the market and talk my ear off. He'd often have his lady friend, a woman he had met in the double A's. First words out of her mouth were, 'I am Ann. I quit drinking.' All the two of them would do is talk about that. And they wondered why I never went to one of the damn meetings in the basement of those churches. They're worse than the Born-Again people.

"Did you hear Elaine's started law school?" he asked as I gave him his change from his weekly Chelsea bun.

"No." Since Daniel was born I hadn't said her name. I was 322 days clean and sober from obsessing about Elaine.

"Nearly 900 applicants and she made it in. My girl, huh?" He must have stood there for twenty minutes telling me how she was going to defend criminals. I thought, how appropriate for her. Not in a mean way. Having been one herself, she would know how they felt. She'd never forget a detail. She would be the one I'd want defending me.

"Say hi to her for me," I said. Ann tried to nickel and dime me until finally I threw in an extra Chelsea bun so they'd be on their way.

It took me about a day to realize when he told me about Elaine I wasn't comparing myself to her. I wasn't jealous. I was happy for her. She was doing better and so was I.

HARRY

Harry's idea of flirting was to try and eat as many of my cookies as he could stuff into his mouth. At first I didn't find it a turn-on. The man would eat everything left over. And stay to the end of market day in order to help me pack up my merchandise and tables. He took to Daniel right away. No matter how much the boy squirmed, Harry would wait until he stopped then buckle him in to his car seat. Daniel and I both started to smile every time we saw him.

I had gotten the low-down on him from the other vendors. He was an Osborne, Helen and Dutch Osborne's son from down the road in Sillsville. Helen had died many years before but Dutch was a terribly violent man and ran the kids right into the ground with his meanness. The market people said Harry was a bit queer. A bit queer didn't mean what it does now. Queer meant he was thinking a little outside of their narrow-minded ways, which made him interesting to me.

Having a baby had taken the flirt out of me. I had been so brazen with men when they were running away from me.

But Harry scared me. He looked as though if I gave him any encouragement he'd never leave. I did do it differently with him in regards to sex. We waited for six weeks, which is like living in dog years when you're in heat. When I finally gave him the go-ahead, he carried me into the bedroom and said he wanted to make love with the lights on. That was almost a deal breaker. I told him he could just go on home if he expected nudity. But he didn't listen to me. He unbuttoned his shirt and dropped his pants. There, running down the front of both legs, were the biggest burn scars I'd ever seen. His leg looked like melted candles.

"My mother was running me a bath and put me in the tub. When she left to get me a towel, the door locked behind her. The water poured in on top of me. I was just three years old so I didn't have the sense to get out. I stood there in the tub screaming, watching hot water come up around my legs. She turned on all the other faucets to divert the pressure. Finally the firemen came and chopped down the door, but by the time they got to me, I was left like this."

He said it matter of fact, like that was the way of it. Then he took me on the bed and undressed me. My skin was red and inflamed. The good life hadn't cured me of that. I tried covering up. After all a scarred man's body looks heroic like he had done battle with life but a woman's body with marks on it is ugly.

"You look like a cheetah," he said.

"You are so full of shit," I said. I placed the sheet over myself, but he took it away once more. He kissed each spot, tenderly.

Daniel and I moved in with him a couple of years later and despite the numerous Catholic Register articles mailed to us by Alberta, we never got hitched. Still, he is a wonderful partner and father. When he was little, Daniel would crawl on Harry's back, sleep all night on top of him like he was an opossum. I didn't think I'd ever get that kid out of our bed.

Harry had one glaring fault that I chose to overlook: he was a farmer. What vengeful God up there would do that to me? The only reason I even moved in was he didn't have livestock, just cash crops. The man loved earth in a way I'd never seen. He couldn't wait to get his hands in the dirt. Digging made him solid. Two years ago he planted two fields full of wheat without pesticides. One field grew perfectly and the other turned to rust. So he gathered up the bad seed and put it in one can, and put the good seed in another. But by planting time, he had forgotten which can each seed was in. This meant that he had to wait another year to see which one would grow right.

His love didn't save me from the hate I had on for myself. I was doing well compared to where I had been but some days it would come out of nowhere, just hit me in the face and nothing I could do or say felt right. I focused on my ugly body, on my father dying so young. I hated Harry's happiness. He shopped for it while I looked for trouble. I think I was born discontented. I was always looking for a place I didn't fit.

My unhappiness came out in harshness. I did crafts and cooked and sewed and tried to get everybody to be happy. I'd try to do things with my son nobody else would've ever thought possible. It seemed I could be a good mother for about fourteen hours but it was always that last ten minutes before bed that got me. I'd resort to screaming. Daniel would be crying 'bad Mommy' and the rage would boil. I wanted to slug him but I didn't.

During these episodes, Harry would tell me to relax but telling me to relax only made me madder. In fact the more I got angry the more I convinced myself I was doomed.

One night I was lying in bed having a pout. Exhausted by the events of the day, I told Harry he could put the kid to bed. Up in my bedroom I was lying there, sweating. It was boiling hot. The kind of summer night you couldn't catch a breath.

Everything was plain miserable.

The bedroom window was open. I could hear Harry talking. I looked out and there they were the two of them. Instead of heading into the house they were heading away from it. They were walking down the driveway toward the ditch that was as dry as a bone. Daniel was about three so he was asking 'why this' and 'why that'?

When they got to the edge of the road, Harry started showing him some baby turtles.

I sat up. I was just about to yell 'put that child to bed', but the tenderness of his voice stopped me.

"See the mama turtle? She crawled out of the swamp two miles down the road." Harry pointed for Daniel, to show him how far she had come with her slow turtle legs. "She dragged herself out of the swamp, came across the highway and went all the way down this country road, went all that way and didn't get hit."

"Why?"

"She laid her eggs right here. Then she took off."

"But why?" Daniel asked again.

"That's just what Mama turtles do."

After Daniel was fast asleep Harry walked into our room. As he sat down on the edge of the bed to take off his pants, I said, "That mother turtle is stupid. Those baby turtles are going to get hit."

"What?"

"The mother turtle! The mama turtle leaves them on the side of the road and now they're going to get hit by a car."

"What are you going on about?"

"After all that journey, she could have taken them four inches further before she took off."

"That's what turtles do."

"Well the turtle didn't do enough."

"She did her job."

"Four more inches and the babies would've been safe."

"Well it's a cruel world in nature. It's survival of the fittest."

"It doesn't make it right."

"Maybe the turtle is being too hard on herself."

"Maybe the turtle should have some standards."

"Tammy, go to sleep. You'll feel better in the morning" He turned over and put his ass toward me; which meant there was no more discussion for the night.

I went downstairs and made some warm milk and cinnamon. A slight deviation on Nana Mary's remedy. Just like my ancestors I was sitting up in the middle of the night figuring out my life while people slept.

Everybody in my family had been trying to move forward since the famine back in the old country. From moving across the ocean to moving across the river, we'd all been moving somewhere. Everybody was inching along. We were all doing our best. But I still didn't know why, when we put up with what we did, we couldn't put up with it a little longer. I mean Lillian left. Dolly left. I left. King left. Why did we have to drop each other so close to the safety zone? I wrote this all in a letter to Elaine because that's what I did when I had things to work out. It was like Alberta talking to the cows. I didn't expect answers. It's just if I wrote a letter to her I could figure out what I was thinking. I would explain it all to her and when I was done I'd read it over and rip it up because she didn't need to be reading my asinine piece of drivel.

Then I went back upstairs and woke Harry up.

"What do you want, Tammy?"

"I want you, Harry." Then I made him put his arms around me and all night long we held each other like star-crossed lovers.

SUMMER KITCHEN

It takes a long time to get redemption. By the time I was 29 I had three boys. Daniel spoiled us, being such a cute one so we were lulled into a false sense of security. The next two were hellions coming out of the gate. So there will be no more babies. With a farm in constant need of repair, and a man you had to watch full time or he'd do something crazy, I should have been satisfied. But I'd get an itch and start looking to raise hell. I'd want to tear something up. I'd tell Harry I wanted to leave. I'd say I have to go Harry, like telling him would stop me somehow. But he thought it was perfectly normal to want to run away from him.

"Well I want to run too, Tammy."

"Sometimes you drive me crazy, Harry."

"You're no hell to live with either." It may not sound romantic but it cracked me up that he could be so honest, and somehow saying it to each other would settle me again.

The only problem was after my disclosure he'd think he had to do something to keep me entertained. He'd come up with one hair-brained project after another. He thought we should home-school. What a stupid idea that was. The only reason my three boys are still breathing on this earth is because that bus comes daily.

The reason I own a bakery is because he went to town and put an offer in on the China Doll. I could have brained him.

"You had no right to do that, Harry."

"Tammy calm down. I put an offer in on it. That's all."

"I don't want to be there in town. It reminds me of the past." He wanted me to stop being so dramatic. Harry didn't know half of it. He thought I was just some troubled teenager who'd exaggerated what partying I'd done. "It gives me a hangover just saying the word China Doll."

"We'll fix it up so you won't recognize it. You can paint it or clean it. Just do something." Harry walked off. There was no way I was going to be another family member fixing up some store that they didn't want. So I drove into town to tell Chan that Harry had spoken out of turn. As I parked the truck in front of the China Doll I was flooded with memory.

The Cadillac Tavern was no longer there. It had burnt down. The China Doll was two streets over from the market but I hadn't driven down that street in years.

Chan and I were still close. We'd have a good yak now and then but kids and farming kept me busy.

When I walked in he was sitting at the counter still reading the Bible as if nine years hadn't passed. No one was in the place. It was hard to tell if this was because of the drug scandal or just the fact he never fixed anything up. It was filthy. The fish were still swimming around in circles like nothing was ever going to get better for them.

When he saw me he insisted on making me an egg roll. I pushed a hole and poured the sauce in as we sat in the booth at the front. I took in his aging face. His hair was salt and pepper. Laugh lines were now permanent wrinkles.

"Harry spoke out of turn saying I'd want to buy this

place."

"What wrong with place?"

"Nothing. I love it."

"You love it, you buy it. I want to retire."

"Chan, you'll never retire."

"Not retire, but retire. See, eating Chinese dinners on way out. People do take out now. See I got plan." He stood in the middle and drew an imaginary line down the centre of the restaurant. "So I do take-out over here. You do baking over there, where the booths are. I be on one side and you be on the other."

"I don't have the money."

"No money needed. I have money. You be Chan's partner. I front you and you pay me when you can. If it works out you make money. I make money. If not I make you go back to church and pray." Chan winked.

So began *Chan to Go* and *The Summer Kitchen Bakery*.

Chan's side stayed the same, but we put a brick wall down the middle with two huge convection ovens on my side so customers could see me making everything. All the ingredients and baking accoutrement were stored in the original kitchen. Although it was technically on his side I would never be there at the same time he was anyway. I opened at 6:00 AM from Tuesday to Saturday.

I made the *Summer Kitchen* look like the one back home. The colours and even some of the pictures on the wall were the same. The floors were all stripped back to natural wood. Without the linoleum they were on such a slope that people felt like they were walking on a hill. I bought some old farm tables and covered them with oilcloths. I went to an inheritance sale and managed to get two red pumps for the bathrooms. People could pump them even though we were hooked up to the town water. Every kid that came in there spent more time in the bathroom slopping water than they did eating. The only difference was Alberta wasn't there spraying fly bomb. . For good luck I put Nana's plastic guard dog at the front by the door.

The fish were put on Chan's side of the store. My side had so much light pouring in they'd have died from the shock. I broadened my offerings from what I'd been doing at the market. Pies were still my biggest selling item, but I added many desserts that needed refrigeration. I had to stop calling things squares, no one ate them by that name. The dollies, butterscotch dots, Queen Elizabeth cake, tomato soup cake; I made ten different types of drop cookies so people could mix and match their dessert choices I used the same take out containers that Chan had used with the little wire handles. I put them in refrigerated cupboards with glass doors so customers could see what was there. I had "a take one, steal one, free" deal so people could pop things in their mouths, guilt-free.

I left for work by four am. I'd look at my new store and think 'how did I ever get so lucky?' There was a time in the past I would've been heading home at that hour. I loved being up and half the day's work complete just as others were going off to work. Not working nine to five kept me on the outside enough I didn't feel I'd conformed.

Two years in and business was good. It was shortly after the Saturday morning rush when the phone rang. Alberta was on the other end, letting me know Elaine was finally tying the knot.

"Good for her."

"It's about time. Apparently she's marrying some mucky muck with the O.P.P. You know, we should give her a shower."

"Alberta. I don't think Elaine would want that."

"I know you don't believe in weddings but we do and all the other nieces got one." Alberta had a rulebook for how things were to be done. We gave showers. We gave gifts. Then we wrote down the presents in a book so you'd know who you should thank.

"I just don't think she'll go for it."

"Actually, I already asked her and she said she'd be okay with it."

"Okay. I'll see if I can make it. I'll definitely go in on a gift."

"Well we thought we'd have it at your place. The bakery. You've got room and that way nobody has to clean their house."

"No. It wouldn't work here. It's just been too long."

"It's water under the bridge, Tammy. The two of you were so close, two peas in a pod and well, she's smartened up a lot." Alberta was sure Elaine had been the bad influence. She had rewritten the part about me cracking up and being a drunk. She referred to my time in the hospital as the time I was 'nervous'. People are never as impressed by your breakdowns as you are.

"We could do it after the long weekend," she continued. "The kids will be back in school and you don't have to buy her a gift if you're the host. And we'll help out. Launa and I will pay you the cost of the bread and the baking goods. Now we wouldn't cover your labour unless you insisted, but what I am saying there would be no out of pocket money."

She went on so much I said I'd do it, just to shut her up.

That's how the big shower got underway. Everybody wanted to have a say. Marley wanted the whole family to come for a Jack and Jill but I didn't want men there. I'd have to invite Harry and that would mean my boys would be running around like hooligans. Then we'd have to deal with Boots, and Elaine's husband to be, this guy called Pat Welland. He was an only child and if we let him in there with the men, there would yelling, talking politics and such. He'd be scared of our brood and run off. Then she'd end up blaming me for being an old maid. I didn't want to be responsible for that.

I wanted an old fashioned girl's shower. There would be no crass games like they had at some of the cousin's showers.

That game where they tie a wiener around the bride-to-be's waist and she had to try to maneuver it into a jar, or a theme shower for the boudoir,or dressing up in a bridesmaid dresses. We would do a traditional party. We'd get the guests to write down their marriage advice. Even though we all knew sweet shit about marriage, it would keep the awkward conversation at bay. There would be no time for Nana to ask about Elaine's jail time if her mouth was full of small pinwheel sandwiches. There would be coffee with sugar cubes, and black tea served in teacups that we'd hold daintily with our pinkies in the air. I wanted Elaine to feel welcomed.

I started off telling myself I would keep it simple, but in the end I opted for perfection. It was psychotic. I had matching everything; pink and blue streamers, everywhere. *The Summer Kitchen* looked like a bridesmaid on acid had decorated it. I baked and baked all night long. When the day arrived I was a nervous wreck.

The aunts showed up in A-line skirts and sallow skin; they were all starting to look alike. Then the once-perfect cousins arrived. Suddenly life had made them quite fat. It was impossible not to notice how dull they were. Nana moved the platters away from them because they would've eaten us out of house and home.

When the honored guest pulled up everybody said shush and they hid. When she came in they all jumped up and said surprise. Even though she knew all about it, Elaine stood in the doorway and smiled like it was a shock.

On her arm was a small frail woman with a cane. It was Lillian. She was so thin that if a wind had come up it would've blown her over. We hadn't invited her but of course she was welcomed. Elaine had gone up to Toronto to get her. Dolly was long gone but Lillian still lived there in a basement apartment in the centre of the city. She looked like she should've been in a nursing home.

It was shocking to see how much Elaine looked like her

mother. When I listened to their voices I had a hard time telling them apart. Lillian wasn't really there; her mind had moved on but nobody bothered to tell her body.

I held back until they made their way through the receiving line of pawing relations. When Elaine and I saw each other she walked very deliberately toward me. There was a quiet about her I didn't recognize. Time or jail had softened her. She was still a looker with her black hair done up in a bun but now she looked wise.

The last thing I wanted to do was start crying, so I offered a piece of my killer lemon pie and decaffeinated tea but she wasn't much for desserts anymore, or so it seemed, for she pushed the crust around on the plate. We ate this and that. The guests chatted amongst themselves about men and how they weren't much good. She asked me if we could go back for a smoke. We sat on the fire escape as if no time had passed.

"You've made the place look great, "she said.

"Thanks."

"Tam, you were always the clever one." I felt sick when she said it.

"No, I wasn't."

"Yes, you were very clever," she said. "God, remember that stinking pig?"

"Oh my God, it reeked."

"I am sorry," she said it so quickly I wasn't sure I heard right.

"Sorry?"

"For not coming to see you after everything went down."

"Well, you were indisposed," I said.

"I meant when I got out," she said. "I had to leave. I couldn't figure it out coming back here so I just kept moving forward, you know?"

"I know."

"Everything I was doing was so wrong. That's why I

called the cops."

"I heard that...but I don't understand. I don't get why you did that."

"When Chan came back and told me you were in hospital, I felt such shame I'd done that to you, that everything had gotten so out of control. I just pulled the plug on the whole operation."

"Because I was ill?"

"I felt bad about it all."

"So you called the cops?"

"It was a desperate moment. When they burst through the door, it felt like a relief that it was over. I hadn't thought it through. If I told on Gordy I would have gotten killed, but telling on myself wasn't bright either."

"You laid on the sword."

"I didn't have a clue, what I was agreeing to. Fourteen months with some of those women. You wouldn't believe their hair."

"Hair?"

"Yes. Ugly-prison hair. Worse than a nun's hairdo."

"Really?"

"They all get the same hair cut. It's sick really. What a wake up call. Everybody in jail says it's not their fault. They never forgive anybody."

"You forgave Boots."

"No I didn't. I just wanted him to do well, for once. There's a big difference. Your Dad was the only Dad I had and when he died, Boots was the only one left. I guess I was just trying to make it hurt less."

"I guess we all were. I know exactly what you mean."

She continued, "We were in over our heads. Big time."

"Big time."

"I didn't know shit. But you, you could tell everything was going on with that Eye thing."

"My kids have beaten it out of me."

"I never meant to hurt you Tammy. I never ever did."

"Hey, I know that. I never meant to hurt you."

"You were good to me."

"No Elaine, I wasn't. I judged everything you did."

"I know. I know that. But so did everybody. Everybody judged me, but at least you kept coming back."

"Well you can't cure stupid." I snorted. This made her laugh.

I was tempted to hug her but we weren't huggers and it would have been pushing it, so I punched her in the shoulder and she stamped out her smoke. As we moved inside I said,

"I dug up Reg."

"I know."

"You do?"

"Everybody knows. It's a small town. Why did you do that?"

"I don't know. "

"People do strange shit when they're loaded. I can't believe the Cadillac Tavern burnt down." That's Elaine for you. She changes the subject and moves on. We went back inside. I showed her to her spot at the head of the table with the big captain's chair decorated in multi-coloured streamers. She wore a paper plate hat, with bows on it while I wrote down the gifts she received so she could write the "proper" thank you. There we were: a lawyer, a baker. Two cousins sitting there at a wedding shower like we had been groomed for this moment our entire lives.

That night I was too tired to move. I sat on my back deck watching my boys swimming in our above ground pool. It required monstrous upkeep but they didn't like the river with all the weeds and mud squishing beneath their toes. I don't swim at all any more. As the kids and Harry screamed, "Look at me," I stared across the water to the place where I grew up, where Elaine and I swam in the water diving for underwater treasures. Innocent wet legs and soggy bathing suits with drooping bottoms, we were closer than sisters. We lived and breathed each other for years never really knowing who the other one was. That's the way it is when you live next to family. No one knows anyone. You do something stupid and it takes twenty years for them to update their files. You can't seem to see family until you get away from them. Life moves you forward to a new spot and there you are standing in some sweet deliciousness your imagination could never could have created. It took every ounce of restraint for me not to not call her and tell her what I was thinking.

The timing wasn't right. I would just end up agreeing to make her wedding cake and doing stuff I'm not ready to do yet. I need to let it sit a bit. I got up to go inside, turning off the lamp with the shade the traveling salesman had given us. Though it was Elaine who had asked him for it, that shade with our farm illuminated. It had become my treasure, one of the few things that came, unaffected into the present.

The past disappeared into night. I lay in bed smoking my cigarette, my finger tracing her name on my bare stomach.

ABOUT THE AUTHOR

DEBORAH KIMMETT is a comic, performer, and writer. Having authored 3 books of comedic essays and 5 plays, (Miracle Mother being nominated for a Governor General Award) she tours North America with her solo shows. Kimmett appears regularly on radio and TV and teaches creative workshops online and in person. She lives in Toronto.

Made in the USA
Charleston, SC
26 August 2016